The Mystery
of the
Phantom

Your

ROBIN KANE

Library

Robin Kane

THE MYSTERY OF THE PHANTOM

by Eileen Hill

illustrated by
Sylvia Haggander

WHITMAN PUBLISHING COMPANY · Racine, Wisconsin

CONTENTS

1.

A New Neighbor

ROBIN KANE dashed out of the side door of Cypress Junior-Senior High School moments after the dismissal bell had sounded. Shielding her eyes from the sudden blaze of the sun, she looked expectantly in the direction of the tennis courts.

"Hey, Sue!" she called out to one of her friends waiting in line to board the big yellow school bus at the curb. "Have you seen Mindy?"

"She's probably still down at the courts. When I left she was practicing her serve. It's been giving her a lot of trouble lately. She'd better step on it or she'll miss the bus." With a wave of her hand, Sue swung up the steps. "So long, Robin. See you tomorrow."

Robin started down the path leading to the athletic field and the tennis courts, her books clutched tightly in her arms. Then suddenly she stopped short. Pushing the short brown curls back from her forehead, she plopped down on a stone bench in the shade of a huge live oak. *Maybe,* Robin thought, *I shouldn't interrupt her practicing.* Robin could beat Mindy at tennis any day, and when she did, Mindy all too often threw down her racket in anger and vowed she would never play that "silly old game" again.

It's not that I'm a better player than Mindy, Robin mused. *It's just that she gets so impatient and expects it all to come easily without any effort on her part.*

Robin traced a circle with the toe of her loafer in the gravel of the path.

Well, if she's decided to work at it, I'm not about to interrupt her, not even if I haven't seen her since Friday, Robin thought to herself.

She was so preoccupied that when Mindy, a few minutes later, crept up from behind and put her fingers over her friend's eyes, Robin let out an involuntary "Eeeek!"

"Guess who?" Mindy said gruffly.

"From the sound of your voice I'd say you're the tall, dark, handsome stranger I dream about, but the faint scent of that special cologne of yours gives you away, Mindy," Robin said with a chuckle.

"You really *are* a detective, Robin." Mindy tossed her long blond hair over her shoulder and sat down. "You don't miss a thing, do you?"

"Not old Keen-eyed Kane!" Robin laughed. "But listen, I've got oodles to tell you. What do you think happened this weekend while you and your father were away?"

"Don't tell me I missed something," Mindy moaned. "I *knew* I would, but Daddy was so anxious for Michael and me to drive down to the Inn at Monterey with him, we just couldn't say no. He's been working so hard getting ready to shoot his new picture, he needed a rest."

"He has been looking sort of tired," Robin said. "I'm glad you went with him. I never can decide if he sometimes forgets to include you in his plans because he's so busy or because he thinks he'd be interrupting some of *our* doings."

"Probably a little of both," Mindy answered soberly. Then her face brightened. "Now, quick! Tell me what happened. Did that genius brother of yours discover gold in some of those rocks he's forever bringing home?"

"No, the Kanes haven't suddenly become rich, I'm sorry to say," Robin replied with a shake of her head. "Daddy still has to turn out his weekly batch of comic strips. 'Family Scene' still has to bring in our family bacon. No, it's about our new neighbor."

Robin stopped suddenly. She looked toward the

school driveway and then at her watch.

"Look, Mindy, you've missed the bus, so why not come on home with me for dinner; then we'll have time to get caught up on all the news."

"Honestly, Robin Kane, you're the worst tease!" Mindy impatiently tossed her tennis racket onto the lawn. "I know it's no use my begging you to tell me anything until you're good and ready, so I'll curb my impatience. But you should know by now that you don't have to bribe me to visit your house. I'm always glad of an excuse to go home with you. *Our* house is so, well, sort of lonely since—"

Tears welled up in Mindy's large brown eyes as they still sometimes did even two years after the death of her mother. She quickly wiped them away, took a deep breath, and forced a smile.

"I know," Robin said sympathetically. "It's bound to be lonely with your father having to be away so much, but I guess that's part of being a great producer-director."

"Yes, that and having to live in a great ark of a house." Mindy sighed as the two girls gathered up their belongings and started down the path to the school gate.

"Why, Melinda Hunter, it's a beautiful house!" Robin exclaimed. "That wonderful heated swimming pool and all those lovely rooms and everything!"

"It may be beautiful, but I'd trade it any day for yours," Mindy answered in a low voice. "Yours is a home, not just a house, although I must say Manuela does her best to take care of us, and Michael—" Mindy's voice again trailed off into silence as she thought of another problem her mother's death had caused.

"I know what you were going to say," Robin said warmly. "Michael has more responsibilities than any sixteen-year-old ought to have. Right?"

"You're *so* right, Robin. I don't think Daddy realizes how much he depends on my brother."

"Well, come to think of it, we *all* depend a lot on Mike, don't we? He's pretty special, you know."

A faint blush crept up Robin's cheek as she said this, and Mindy noted that she changed the subject rather abruptly.

"How about stopping in at the Cupboard?" Robin said. "You can phone Manuela from there. By the way, why don't you ask Mike to come for dinner, too? Then he can drive you home in the station wagon."

"A good idea, but are you sure your mother won't mind having two hungry kids descend on her without notice?"

"Heavens, no!" Robin cried. "You know Mom! What's two more when she has five Kanes to feed, plus Tig and Tramp, to say nothing of the other animal guests my softhearted little sister is forever bringing home?"

The Cupboard, a favorite gathering place for the young people of Pacific Point, was crowded, as it usually was after school hours. As the girls made their way to the rear where the phone booth was wedged into a corner, they heard a voice call to them from the patio.

"Hey, Robin, Mindy, come on out a sec!"

It was Robin's brother, Kevin. He was only a year older than Robin, but being fourteen, and now in senior high, he sometimes acted as though he were the only person who had ever graduated from junior high school. At least Robin occasionally accused him of thinking that.

"Hi, frosh!" Robin called as she approached him. She twisted the button on top of the orange and blue beanie which all first-year classmen were required to wear for a month. "What gives?"

Kevin gave his sister a withering look, which, however, was completely lost on her. Robin's attention had suddenly been caught by a boy on the other side of the table. His reddish hair and broad shoulders under a navy-blue blazer were familiar. She recognized him as the same boy she had seen over the weekend carrying a lot of boxes and luggage into the house near hers—a house which everyone in Pacific Point said was haunted. Her thoughts were interrupted as he stood up and, taking the books from her arms, beckoned her to sit down. This unusual show of courtesy apparently surprised the others at the table as much as it had Robin, for there followed a sudden shuffling of feet and rather awkward attempts at rising to make room for her at the long table.

"Thanks a lot!" she said, smiling at the newcomer as she slid onto the redwood bench. Then, turning to her brother, she added, "Mindy'll be along in a minute. She's phoning Manuela to let her know she's eating at our house tonight."

"Oh, swell!" Kevin said. Then he turned to the new boy. "Robin, meet Joe Turner. Joe, my sister Robin. This is Joe's first day at school. He's a junior this year."

It was quite obvious that Kevin was not only enjoying the chance to introduce an older boy to his sister, but was also proud of exuberant, outgoing Robin. Although she was a lot more casual about her appearance than her friend Mindy, she was nevertheless a warm, attractive girl, and Kevin secretly thought she was tops.

"I knew I'd seen you before," Robin smiled. She held out her hand across the table. "Welcome to Pacific Point, Joe."

It wasn't long before Mindy joined them. Robin felt a little prick of envy when she noticed that Mindy looked as fresh and pretty as the proverbial daisy, despite the tennis practice, the walk from school, and several minutes in a hot phone booth. Her white piqué dress was spotless and her hair smooth and shining.

This time *all* the boys, taking their cue from Joe, clambered to their feet, nearly upsetting the many Cokes and malteds that littered the long table. Joe was introduced to Mindy, and then, miraculously, everyone got seated again without mishap.

"Isn't he the *most?*" Robin whispered to Mindy.

Conversation was buzzing around them. Everyone seemed anxious to find out all about Joe, and he was being besieged with questions. "What's your favorite sport?" "Do you go out for track?" "Do you play any instrument?" "How about amateur theatricals?"

Before Joe finished answering one question, another would be popped at him. Robin began to suspect that the questioners were not so much interested in what Joe did as in tooting their own particular horn so *he* would know what *they* did.

She looked around the table and conceded to herself that it was a rather special group. There at the end was good-looking, talented Ed, last year's lead in the Theater-in-the-Grove production of *May Song*. Next to him was Tony, one of the most popular boys in town despite his penchant for playing practical jokes on his friends. Nearby sat quiet Sam; two of his watercolors had recently been chosen to hang in the local art show. And, yes, there was Kevin, who could sometimes make his guitar sound like Segovia himself. Robin felt she just had to rescue Joe from this interrogation.

Taking her courage in her hands, and hammering on the table with an empty Coke bottle, she shouted, "Hey, all of you! Give Joe a chance! You sound like a bunch of newspaper reporters interviewing the

latest celebrity to reach our fair city."

Everyone laughed, and Joe turned to her with a smile.

"Thanks for throwing me a lifeline, Robin," he said, his dark eyes twinkling. "I'm certainly not a celebrity, but I *am* new to Pacific Point—and to America, for that matter. I came over from England and hitchhiked out here from New York. Now, to try and answer all your questions at once, let's say I'm a jack-of-all-trades and a master of none."

"Oh, come on, Joe!" somebody cried. "You can't get out of it that easily. We'll find your hidden talents in time. Almost everybody in Pacific Point does *something*. Right, gang?"

A chorus of "Right!" echoed back as the group started to break up.

"Why don't you ask him over for dinner tonight?" Robin whispered to Kevin as Joe moved out of ear-shot. "He's cute, and so polite."

"Oh, you girls! All you think about are looks and manners, for pete's sake. Don't you ever think of a guy's brains?" Kevin growled.

"Well, how will we know if his brains measure up to yours if we don't talk to him some more?" Mindy asked, giving Kevin her sweetest smile.

That was enough to win him over, and he hurried out to catch up with Joe, who was already on the street.

"Now, will you please cue me in on the big news,

Robin?" Mindy said impatiently. "I can't wait another minute."

"You've already met him," Robin laughed. "But it's not just that. The interesting thing is that he moved into the old Williams house last Saturday."

"You don't mean that creepy old place that everyone says is haunted, do you?" Mindy's eyes were wide with surprise.

"Yes, I do mean that creepy old place," Robin replied. "I don't think anyone's lived there since old Mrs. Williams died."

"They say she was a witch!" Mindy said, shivering slightly.

"Oh, they say lots of things about her and the house. I remember when I was only eight and Kevin dared me to go over there after dark—alone." Robin stopped, the memory of that night still fresh.

"What happened?" Mindy asked. "You never told me that story before."

"Nothing actually *happened*," Robin said, "but I was sure I saw someone inside when I finally got up close to the window. There was just enough light from the street lamp for me to make out a form on an old sofa."

"Was it a man or a woman?" Mindy asked.

"I don't know. I took one look and grabbed a flower from the jasmine vine and skedaddled for home," Robin answered. "I never could stand the smell of jasmine after that night."

"What an odd thing to do! What ever made you pick flowers at a time like that?" Mindy queried.

"Well, you see, Kevin wanted proof that I had actually gone all the way up to the house. There was a huge red jasmine vine growing over one end of the porch, the only red jasmine anywhere around. So he told me to bring back a flower to prove I'd been there."

"He would! I'll bet *he* never set foot in that eerie place," Mindy said.

"Well, he claims he did, but I wasn't mean enough to demand evidence, as he did."

The two friends had been slowly walking out of the business section of Pacific Point and down the street where Robin lived. When they came to the corner of the pine grove in which lay the Kane's big rambling house, Robin and Mindy squeezed through a small break in the willow-sapling fence surrounding the property and cut across to the patio.

"Anybody home?" Robin called out, throwing her books onto a table near the pool.

She and Mindy were nearly bowled over by Tramp, the Kanes' dog, who, at the sound of a familiar voice, had come bounding out of the house, his one drooping ear flapping wildly. He was joined shortly by Tig, who, with customary feline grace, slowly uncurled her sleek black body, jumped down from the bench where she had been sleeping, and rubbed against Robin's leg.

"Dear Tig! Her heart really belongs to Amy, but every once in a while she'll favor the rest of us with a caress."

Robin knelt down and scratched the big cat under her chin. Tig responded with loud purrs of satisfaction. This brought forth yips of jealousy from Tramp until Robin patted him on the head and told him what a fine dog he was.

Mrs. Kane appeared in the doorway, her dark-rimmed glasses pushed down to the end of her nose, a wood-carving knife in her hand. She greeted the girls warmly. Then she glanced at the sun, which was already low in the sky, and then at her watch.

"Goodness me! How time flies! I began working on a fascinating piece of driftwood and completely lost track of the hour."

"Oh, oh! That means bread and water for supper tonight!" Robin wailed, rolling her eyes and holding her tummy. "And me with important guests, too!"

"Well, it just so happens that I had a premonition this morning that since you and Mindy hadn't seen each other for two whole days, you might be bringing her home tonight, so I took a big casserole of chili con carne out of the freezer." Mrs. Kane put her arm affectionately around Mindy's shoulder.

"Oh, Mom, you're a living doll!" Robin cried. "Will there be enough for two extra boys?"

"Of course, dear. We can always stretch it with a can or two of beans, you know," Mrs. Kane laughed.

"Who else are you expecting?"

"I hope Mike will be down, if he gets through cataloging some rocks he found this weekend," Mindy said. "You know his collection comes before every-thing—that is, everything except your cooking."

"You flatter me, Mindy dear," Mrs. Kane said. "Well, Mike accounts for one, now who's the other?"

At that moment Kevin came bounding onto the ter-race followed by Joe. He slid to a stop inches from the edge of the pool, then, wheeling around, grabbed his new friend by the wrist and led him over to meet his mother.

In the midst of Mrs. Kane's cordial welcome, the ringing of the phone sounded from inside.

"You get it, please, Robin," Mrs. Kane said. "It may be your father calling to say when he will be returning from San Francisco, or Amy wanting to be picked up at Judy's."

Robin dashed into the house only to return a few minutes later to announce, "It's for you, Mindy. Your father—calling from Breakwater."

"Oh, I hoped it might be Daddy!" Mindy cried as she started on a run toward the house.

"You know, Mindy misses her father more than we realize," Mrs. Kane said soberly when Mindy was out of earshot.

"She does," Robin agreed, "and I'm glad Mr. Hunter is trying to draw closer to her and Michael—like the trip to Monterey last weekend, and now taking the time to phone from Breakwater."

When Mindy returned, Robin saw at a glance that something had upset her. Mindy's recently sunny face was overcast and her whole attitude was one of dejection.

"Mindy, what's wrong?" Robin cried, jumping up to meet her friend.

"Daddy called to see if we were all right," Mindy said, "but he sounded rushed and not like himself at all. I finally got him to tell me—" She hesitated before blurting out, "Something happened on the set. I can see why Daddy would be upset!"

She dropped into a chair and hid her face in her hands, unable to say anything more.

2.

A Haunted House

EVERYONE gathered around Mindy, not knowing quite what to do or say. The phone call had
cast a pall over what had started out to be a happy
gathering. Mrs. Kane leaned over and placed her hand
gently on Mindy's shoulder. She started to speak, but
seeing Robin press her finger to her lips and shake
her head, she kept silent, realizing her daughter
wanted to give her friend time to pull herself together. Although Mindy sometimes relished the idea
of being the center of attention, Robin knew in-
stinctively that this was not such an occasion. Mindy

wasn't playacting this time.

"Kevin, why don't you show Joe the Huddle?" Robin suggested, sensing the boys' embarrassment.

"Yeah, come on, Joe, and see our clubhouse," Kevin said quickly, relief in his voice. "Then——"

"Oh, yes," Joe broke in. "That sounds like a good idea, but don't you think it might be better if we left that for another time? I'd best be running along. I mean, wouldn't Mindy rather——"

"Of *course* not, Joe," Mindy said, looking up quickly. "Don't you think of leaving. I'll be all right in a minute."

Good girl, Robin thought to herself as she watched Mindy force a smile.

Kevin and Joe started toward the far end of the patio where a small structure, originally intended for guests, had been converted into a clubhouse and dubbed the Huddle. Mrs. Kane, on the pretext of starting dinner, went inside, leaving the two girls alone.

Robin sat down beside Mindy and put her hand on her arm.

"Now, tell me all about it. What happened?" Her face mirrored her concern.

Mindy straightened up and dabbed her eyes with her handkerchief.

"Well, as I said, Daddy wasn't going to mention what had happened, but I finally wheedled it out of him," she began. "A beautiful articulated fish that plays a big part in his film has disappeared!"

"A what?" Robin asked. "An ar-tic— Whatever in the world is *that?*"

"I'd never heard of one, either," Mindy said. "On the way down to Monterey last Saturday, Daddy stopped off at Breakwater to show us around the place where he's shooting the film. The whole story revolves around this antique fish which Daddy got on loan from a museum in San Francisco."

"It's not a live fish, then?" Robin said.

"No, it is made of gold, about a foot long, with red stones that look like rubies for eyes. The very thin scales of the fish are so cleverly put together that you can make the whole fish wiggle just like a real one. One of the meanings of 'articulated' is 'jointed,' Daddy said. And now it's gone."

"Oh, Mindy, how awful!" Robin cried. "Hasn't he any idea what happened to it?"

"Not the slightest. The fish disappeared sometime between the time we left Breakwater Friday night and this morning."

"Where was it kept?" Robin asked, her mind already busy trying to reconstruct the situation.

"It was in a wooden box, rolled up in a cloth—the kind they use to keep silver from tarnishing—in a little shack Daddy is using as an office," Mindy said. "I'm sure I saw him closing the padlock on the door when we were leaving. Michael was there. I'm sure he will remember, too."

"Here he comes now," Robin said, jumping up at the familiar sound of the bullhorn Michael had installed in the station wagon.

"Why don't you go and tell your mother what's happened while I run out and talk to Mike?" Mindy suggested. "She was a dear to leave us alone to talk, but she's probably dying to know what it's all about."

"Okay," Robin said as she headed for the house. "See you in a minute, Min."

While Kevin had been introducing Joe to the clubhouse with its accumulation of surfboards, water skis, and other paraphernalia, he had been keeping half an eye on Mindy and his sister. When he saw Robin go into the house, he and Joe followed her and reached the kitchen in time to hear the details of the news that had so upset Mindy.

"That *is* a bad piece of luck," Joe said. "Whoever would steal a thing like that?"

"That's what I can't figure out," Robin said as she took a handful of potato chips from the large wooden bowl on the table. "An object like an ar-articulated fish must be very unusual, and I should think the thief would have a hard time selling it. Maybe whoever took it only wanted it for himself, just because it was so beautiful."

"It could always be melted down and the metal sold," Kevin suggested.

"Hmmm, maybe," Robin mused, "but the fish was probably hollow, and I wouldn't think the value of

the gold alone would make it worthwhile for anyone to steal it."

"What other motive would anyone have?" Mrs.
Kane asked. "Could the fish have been misplaced?"

Mindy and her brother came in from the patio
just in time to hear her question. Michael's thin,
freckled face was serious, but a smile lighted his
deep-set brown eyes as he greeted Mrs. Kane and
said hello to Robin and Kevin. After he had been introduced to Joe he turned again to Mrs. Kane.

"Getting back to what you said, Mrs. Kane, that's
my hunch, too. From what Mindy tells me, I feel the
fish may have been misplaced. Everything was pretty
disorganized down at Breakwater because Dad was
in such a hurry to get started."

"Why all the rush?" Robin asked. "I thought Mr.
Hunter had a reputation for taking a long time on
his pictures."

"You're right," Mindy replied. "He's usually ter-
ribly particular about every little detail, but this isn't
a movie, remember. It's a documentary for television,
and he's working against time."

"Yes, it's one of a series about the early Spanish
missions," Michael went on to explain, "and they
were late getting started because Westpark Films didn't
make up their minds about who was to direct it until
a week or so ago."

"But that still doesn't explain why the rush now,"
Robin interrupted.

"Hold your horses," Michael said with a laugh. "I was just coming to that. Dad wants to get this documentary done in time to qualify for a special TV award. That is the real reason for the rush. All the entries have to be submitted by the first of next month."

"Well, I can certainly see why the disappearance of the fish might delay things," Mrs. Kane said, "but perhaps they can shoot some other scenes first— scenes in which the fish doesn't appear—and by that time it may turn up."

"Oh, I do hope so," Mindy sighed. "Daddy had such hopes of making this a— Well, he called it a little gem. He loved the story the minute he finished reading the script." Tears welled up in her eyes.

"And that's not all," she went on in a shaky voice. "Daddy was so eager to make the picture that he arranged to put up the—the end money to finish it."

"The *what?*" Robin asked in amazement. "What on earth is end money?"

"It's a bit technical, Robin," Michael explained gravely. "You see, when a producer has made all the plans for a story to be filmed, like choosing the scriptwriter and hiring the stars, he goes to a bank and arranges for the money to pay all the costs."

"Well, why would your father need this end money you're talking about?" Robin asked. "I'm still confused!"

"So was I," Mindy said understandingly, "until

he explained it to me. It seems the bank wants a guarantee that the picture will actually be finished, so someone outside has to put up the money."

"And it's only used if the picture isn't completed," Michael added, "or if it costs more than the original budget called for."

"I get it," Robin said softly. "Your father guaranteed that the picture would be finished, so if anything happens he'll have to pay it out of his own pocket."

"That's right, Robin," Michael said, his voice troubled, "and in this case it could cost Daddy thousands and thousands of dollars!"

"Well, it certainly is a blow," Mrs. Kane said as she got up from the table to check the oven, "but right now why don't you all try to put it out of your minds for a while? Take a swim while I go over and pick up Amy. Then it will be time for dinner."

"That's a good idea, Mom," Robin said, making an attempt to lighten the spirits of her friends. "Maybe we'll get some other ideas if we just let the whole thing simmer. Come on, everybody! Let's go!"

Kevin lent Joe a pair of trunks. Michael and Mindy each kept an extra suit at the Kanes'—they seemed to swim there more often than in their own pool. Soon they were ready. First the boys dove in from the side of the pool. Then Mindy's perfect swan dive from the board brought cheers from everyone.

"I can't beat *that* kind of performance," Robin

cried as she held her nose and purposely did an awkward backflip into the water.

There was more horseplay and splashing than actual swimming, and when Mrs. Kane returned with Amy she was glad to find that the tensions of the previous hour seemed to have drained away.

"How's my Sug?" Robin called to her little sister. "Come here and meet our new neighbor." She pulled herself up on the side of the pool and beckoned Joe to join her.

"Joe, this is my sister Amy, only we usually call her Sugar because—"

"Because she's so sweet. That's obvious," Joe said as he knelt down in front of Amy and took her two hands in his.

Amy, who was usually shy with strangers, gave Joe a long look and then said softly, "Hello, Joe. Would you care to see my pet hamster?"

"I'd like nothing better, Sugar," Joe answered, and the two walked off, hand in hand, to see her pet.

"Jumpin' cats, can you tie that!" Kevin said, scratching his head. "What's happened to our little Amy?"

"Looks like Joe has made another conquest." Mindy glanced at Robin under her long lashes.

"I wonder what his family's like?" Robin said, ignoring Mindy's attempt to tease her. "I'll bet anything he's got a little sister, too."

"We were so busy talking about the fish, I'm afraid

we were kind of rude to Joe," Mindy said as she shook
the water out of her hair and pounded her ear gently
with the heel of her hand. "Let's try to make up for
it at dinner."

The two girls went inside, leaving Kevin and Michael to wait for Amy and Joe. After they had dressed
they joined Mrs. Kane in the kitchen. Mindy always
said this was her favorite room. The walls of a large
arched area where the stove was placed were covered
with bright Mexican tiles. Handmade pottery and
baskets lined the shelves on either side, and from the
dark beams in the ceiling hung a variety of peppers,
herbs, and gourds. A heavily carved oak table which
Mrs. Kane had bought at an auction stood in the
middle of the room. She had paid very little for it
because it was in such bad repair that no one else
had been interested in it. Mr. Kane had reglued it
and the whole family had worked to remove the old
finish, sand it as smooth as glass, and rub coat after
coat of wax into the wood. Robin, who had often
grumbled at the seemingly endless work that had gone
into it, was now prouder than anyone of the beautiful piece.

"May we eat in here tonight, Mrs. Kane?" Mindy
asked. "I love this room. It always smells so warm
and spicy."

"You can't smell warmth, silly," Robin said, "but
I know what you mean. Mom doesn't care where we
eat, do you, Mom?"

"Anywhere you children want. It makes no difference to me," Mrs. Kane replied.

Robin took some gaily colored straw place mats and the silver from a nearby chest and started to set the table.

"Let's see, we'll let Amy sit here beside Joe," she said, "and, Mindy, you sit on his other side."

"Oh, you're *so* generous," Mindy laughed as she put a goblet at each place, "but I see through your strategy. You're planning to sit opposite so you can see him better. Right?"

"Ah, woe is me!" Robin wailed, clutching her head in a dramatic gesture. "My plot has been discovered."

The boys and Amy trooped in as Mrs. Kane was putting a large brown casserole on the table. Robin supervised the seating with a grin at Mindy as she indicated where she was to sit.

"Mrs. Kane," Joe said, "whatever is in that dish smells absolutely—how do you Americans say it?— out of this world!"

"Why, thank you, Joe. It's really a Mexican dish, rather than American," Mrs. Kane said. "It's made with beans, chili powder, and 'con carne'—that's Spanish for 'with meat.' "

"You don't have this in England?" Mindy asked as she passed a plate of the steaming mixture to Joe.

"I doubt it," Joe replied. "English food, as a rule, is rather simple, you know. Beef or mutton, a 'veg,' and usually trifle for dessert."

"What in the world is trifle?" Kevin asked.

"Actually, it's leftover cake disguised with jelly or some kind of sauce," Joe laughed. "It's really rather ordinary."

"Well, I'd jump at a chance to go to England even if I had to eat trifle three times a day," Robin declared. "Have you lived there all your life, Joe?"

"Practically," he answered with a smile. "My father went over to work for a London newspaper when I was about a year old, so I don't remember living anywhere else. My little sister Beth and my brother Richard were both born in England."

"My Daddy works for a newspaper, too!" Amy chirped. "He draws a comic strip, and we're all in it, only he calls us Muggins and Fatso and Danny. I'm Muggins and Kevin's Danny and—" She gave a quick glance in Robin's direction.

"Yes, I'm Fatso," Robin moaned, "although it beats me why Daddy chose that name for me."

"All you have to do is take a look at some of those old snapshots he took when you were seven. Then you'll know," Kevin said, giving her a gentle poke. "You and I looked like Jack Sprat and his wife in those days."

"And now is your father going to continue in newspaper work in this country?" Mrs. Kane asked when the laughter had subsided.

"Oh, no," Joe said. "I should have told you. I'm the only one who came back to America. You see,

I've always wanted to go to college over here, and my father thought if I went to high school in the States for a couple of years it would make it easier for me."

"How did you happen to land way out here in Pacific Point, Joe?" Michael asked. "It's about as far from London as you could get and still be in the United States."

"Well, my uncle has always lived in California, so Mother wrote him about my wanting to come to America," Joe replied. "He found out that the schools here in Pacific Point were top-hole so he looked around for a place to rent, and ended up with the Williams house. He's something of an authority on architecture and old houses, and that one fascinated him."

"You mean you and your uncle really live in the Haunted House?" Amy asked, her eyes wide with excitement.

"Yes, we really live there, Sugar," Joe said, smiling down at her. "I'll admit it looks dashed spooky, but I've slept there two nights already and haven't seen or heard a sign of a ghost."

The Haunted House was quite different from the others along the street. For one thing, it was much older, dating from the late eighteen hundreds. The builder had come west from New York State along with the thousands of other people who, in 1849, had flocked to California in search of gold. He had made a fortune, not by striking gold, but by trading with the prospectors. He had eventually retired from business, left San Francisco, and moved his family to Pacific Point, which in those days was a very tiny community. He bought a large piece of land and built himself a grand house. It had all the Victorian curlicues, gingerbread trim, and miniature towers that had been the style back in his native state. Now, years later, it stood out in marked contrast to the rambling adobe or stucco Spanish-type dwellings around it.

"We're all glad the house is occupied again after so many years," Mrs. Kane said. "I do want to meet your uncle very soon. The house has always seemed more lonely than spooky to me, as though it were waiting for a family to move in and care for it again."

"Well, there are only the two of us, my uncle and me, batching it together. I hope you *can* meet him," Joe said a little self-consciously. "I haven't had a chance to get to know him very well myself. I guess he's not quite used to having me around."

Robin, sensing Joe's embarrassment, quickly changed the subject.

For dessert, Mrs. Kane produced a large pie. Succulent cherries shining through a golden-brown latticed crust brought squeals of delight from Amy and ohs and ahs from the others. When everyone had finished, Amy, after a gentle hint from her mother, made her good-nights reluctantly and scampered off to bed. Mindy and Robin helped clear the table, and then Michael, after apologizing to Mrs. Kane for seeming to "eat and run," said, "I've got a ton of homework to do, and I'll bet Mindy has, too, so we'd better get going. It'll be hard enough to study with the lost fish on our minds."

3.

Finding a Box

AT MENTION of the fish, Robin, who had been
unusually quiet during the meal, turned from
the chest where she had been replacing the place mats.

"I've been racking my brain all through dinner to
think of who would do such a thing, but I can't make
any sense out of it."

"Did Dad notify the police or the museum?" Michael asked Mindy.

"I meant to tell you about that," Mindy said.
"Daddy has kept it a secret so far, from everybody
except us. I guess he's hoping the fish will turn up

before he has to report it and start a lot of unfavorable publicity."

The group started to break up. Robin, motioning to Kevin, said, "Come on, we'll walk you out to the Heap."

Tramp, who had been sleeping under the table, suddenly came to life at the familiar words, "Come on," and scrambled toward the door, nearly knocking Robin over in his eagerness to go along.

"I parked the Heap out near the road so it wouldn't be in anyone's way," Michael said.

"Or so it wouldn't disgrace the Kanes' driveway," Mindy laughed.

"What, may I ask, is this Heap you're all talking about?" Joe asked as they walked down the curving driveway to the street.

"It's the smoothest automobile in California," Michael replied proudly. "I've spent the better part of four years bringing it to its present state of perfection."

This brought groans from the others, although they actually adored the old station wagon which had carried them on so many outings—to the beach, the mountains, and Rancho Lucia. There was still enough daylight left for Joe to be able to inspect the car.

"It's a humdinger!" he exclaimed after Michael had lifted the hood to reveal the motor he had rebuilt.

"It may be a humdinger up there in the business end," Robin said, "but wait until you see the interior! Mindy, we'll have to patch up the front seat before all the stuffing comes bursting through and—"

She left the sentence unfinished, for as she opened the door and leaned inside she noticed a brown carton on the driver's seat. It was covering the hole she had been about to show Joe.

"More of Mike's rocks, I suppose," she muttered. "Don't you and Kevin ever get tired of collecting these hunks of stone?"

"What are you talking about?" Michael asked, coming around to the side of the car. "The only rocks around here are in that pretty head of yours."

"Well, what's this, then?" Robin ignored the back-handed compliment and took out the box for Michael to see.

"Never saw it before in my life," he said emphatically. "Watch out, Sherlock Holmes. It may be a bomb!"

He jumped back in pretended alarm.

"Oh, Mike, don't be ridiculous!" Robin said scornfully. Nevertheless she held the carton close to her ear and shook it gently.

"Hear anything?" Mindy asked. "Does it tick?"

"Not a sound. I'll bet it's a surprise for your birthday."

"But that's weeks away," Mindy answered.

"May I be bold enough to suggest that you two girls might solve this mystery by simply opening the box?" Kevin said in a superior tone. "Do you always have to play detective?"

"It's *not* play, and you should be glad your sister *has* a sixth sense about mysteries, Kevin Kane," Mindy said defiantly.

"Oh, come off it, you two," Robin said, taking the box and trying to undo the cord with which it was tied.

"Here, let me give you a hand," Michael said. He knelt down beside Robin, broke the string, and lifted the cover.

The box was lightly stuffed with shredded newspaper which Robin started to pull out eagerly. Heads were pressed close together as the others bent over to watch. Tramp ran frantically around the outside of the circle, finally pushing his way through and sticking his cold nose in Robin's hand.

"Oh, Tramp Kane, it's nothing for you. Be a good dog and go away," Michael said, giving him a gentle nudge. Then Robin, reaching the bottom of the carton, lifted out a second smaller box made of wood.

"Oh, Robin," Mindy cried. "It's just like the box the fish was in. Hurry! Open it!"

No one said a word as Robin undid the brass hook and lifted the cover. Inside was the brown flannel cloth in which the fish had been wrapped, but the fish was missing.

"Oh, no!" Robin cried, disappointment quickly sweeping away the elation she had felt on finding the box.

She leaned dejectedly against the car. What did the

box in the Heap mean? Who could have put it there, and when? Where was the fish? Everyone began asking questions at once; they all looked to Robin for the answers.

"I don't *know!*" she snapped, momentarily impatient with them as well as herself. "Let me *think!*"

"Yes, give Robin a chance," Michael said. "Finding the box may have a lot of implications. We'll all have to do some heavy thinking."

"Implications?" Mindy repeated. "You mean someone may be trying to make it look bad for you and me?"

"No." Michael's answer came slowly as he pondered Mindy's question. "I don't think that's it, because no one would be foolish enough to think *we'd* steal the fish."

"I sort of know what Mike's getting at," Robin said. "The box was obviously planted in the Heap while we were all at dinner. Maybe the thief wanted to draw attention away from Breakwater, and he wanted the box to be found by someone who knew it had contained the fish."

"Then it must be someone who is familiar with the Hunter family," Michael added.

"Why? Because he knew the Heap is yours?" Mindy queried.

"Yes," her brother answered, "and he might even be aware of the fact that our two families are very close friends."

"That's a thought," Kevin said. "Then, if he was looking for the Heap and didn't find it at the Hunters', he'd figure it might be at our house."

"This is all very funny," said Robin, who had been listening intently to the talk around her. "I mean, funny-peculiar, and not funny-ha-ha. Come to think of it, why would anyone assume Mindy and Mike knew about the fish if Mr. Hunter hasn't said anything to anyone at Breakwater?"

"You've got a point there," Michael said, "because there wasn't a soul around when Dad showed us the fish."

"It certainly proves one thing," Mindy said positively. "The fish wasn't mislaid. It was stolen!"

"You're absolutely right," Robin agreed. "I think that you and Mike ought to take the box right home with you and call your father."

"Okay, let's get this stuff cleaned up," Michael said, starting to gather up the paper and repack the carton.

"Let me know what develops," Robin urged them as they got into the Heap. "I don't like the looks of this at all!"

Michael turned the car around and headed for the seacoast and the Hunter mansion. Mindy, holding the box tightly in her arms, looked grim, as though she, like Robin, felt there was more to the incident of the lost fish than either of them knew at the moment.

As the red glow of the taillights faded away in the

distance, Joe shook his head. "My goodness!" he exclaimed. "This has certainly been an exciting day. Are things always as lively as this around here?"

"Thank heavens, no!" Robin answered as the three walked toward the old Williams house. "Usually we lead very quiet lives."

"Oh, yeah?" Kevin jeered. "I suppose it was very quiet when your favorite horse, Nugget, got lost, and you and Mindy were almost kidnapped by El Gato. Very, very quiet!"

"Kidnapped by El Gato!" Joe exclaimed in amazement. "Who on earth is El Gato?"

"He happens to have been one of the most notorious cattle rustlers in today's West," Kevin replied. "El Gato is Spanish for The Cat. Now, thanks to my sister, he's behind bars."

"I thought cattle thieves were as old-fashioned as cowboys and Indians," Joe said. "Don't tell me there are still live ones around here."

"I guess El Gato and his gang were about the last of the real bad men," Kevin said. "The Indians are mostly on reservations, but the cowboys are still around."

"You'll have to come down to Rancho Lucia with us," Robin said eagerly, "and see the *vaqueros*—that's Spanish for cowboys—for yourself. Then you can see Nugget, too. He's the most beautiful horse in the whole world!"

By the time Kevin had finished telling Joe how his

sister had brought about the capture of El Gato and recovered Nugget, they were in front of the old Williams house.

"Sooner or later I'll probably get used to the idea of someone living here," Robin said, hugging her shoulders, "but this house still gives me the creeps!"

By now it was quite dark. The streetlight cast a pale and ghostly glow over the old iron fence and massive gate. As they looked through the tangle of shrubbery surrounding the house, Robin caught sight of a faint light in one of the upper windows.

"Is that your room?" she asked Joe.

"No, that's Uncle George's study. He decided to take the tower room so he'd have plenty of privacy for his writing. Sort of an ivory tower, I'd say." Joe chuckled as he said this. Then, pointing to the far wing of the house, he said, "I chose the old library over there for my digs. Right tidy it is, too, now that I've moved in a cot to sleep on. There's a big old fireplace that reminds me of home, and also stacks of books."

"So your uncle's an author," Robin said eagerly. "Then he should love living in Pacific Point. There are all kinds of talented people here—writers and artists and composers. What sort of books does he write?"

"Well, as a matter of fact, this is the first one he's ever done," Joe replied slowly, pulling at his ear, "and at the rate he's going it may be his last. He told me he started studying California architecture several years ago, but he has just now gotten around to writing the book."

"He must work at about the same speed I do when I have to do a theme for English," Kevin said with a laugh.

"Your trouble is that you always leave it till the last minute," Robin chided. "My brother is a real putter-offer, Joe, unless it's something he really wants to do. Then he's a ball of fire."

"Holy cow! That reminds me, I have a paper due tomorrow," Kevin cried. "Come on, Sis. So long, Joe. See you tomorrow."

"Cheers, you two, and thanks for everything," Joe answered with a wave as he turned in at the gate.

As soon as they got home Kevin went to his room to begin his homework, but Robin lingered in the kitchen to tell her mother about finding the box. Mrs. Kane listened intently, her face mirroring Robin's own concern.

"I do wish your father were here," she said when Robin had finished. "I don't like the sound of this! It—it's frightening."

Robin poured herself a glass of orange juice and, after saying good night to her mother, headed down the long hall to her bedroom. She undressed slowly, thinking over the strange events of the day. After putting on her favorite blue robe, she curled up on the window seat and opened her math book, but try as she might she couldn't keep her mind on the assignment. The numbers danced in front of her eyes. She found herself doodling the outlines of strange fish in the spaces where the answers to the problems should have gone.

Why wasn't I more careful with the box? she chided herself. *Why didn't I examine the shredded newspaper? There may have been fingerprints on the wooden box. Now, after we all handled it, any prints are sure to be smudged.*

Question followed question in her mind. Robin snapped her book shut in disgust and jumped up. She paced up and down her room, finally coming to a stop in front of her dressing table. Leaning over, she pressed her face close to the mirror, her brow wrinkled, her lips pursed.

"Robin Kane, you're a dope, a freckle-faced dope!" she said vehemently. "And *you* dream of becoming a detective!"

At that moment, hearing the phone ringing, she rushed to the door and opened it in time to hear her mother say, "Hold on, Mindy. I'll get her."

"Here I come, Mom," Robin called out. "Oh, jiminy crickets, I certainly hope nothing more has gone wrong."

She felt tense as she took the phone from her mother's hand, but she gradually relaxed as she listened to the voice at the other end of the wire. Then, holding the phone away, she said, "Mom, is it all right if I drive down to the ranch with Michael and Mindy tomorrow? Mr. Hunter wants us to meet him there for dinner."

Mrs. Kane thought a minute before answering, weighing any possible danger against Robin's ability to take care of herself and Michael's sense of responsibility for Robin and his sister.

"I don't see why not," she said finally, "so long as you get your homework done and don't take any chances."

Robin, knowing her mother was thinking about her recent impulsive ride into the hills after El Gato, promised to be careful. Her spirits lightened as she and Mindy made plans for the next day. When the conversation was ended she put her arms around her mother and held her tight.

"You know, Mom, I couldn't bear to have anything happen to the Hunters. They're just like my own family."

"I know how concerned you are, dear, but I sometimes wish you weren't so bent on unraveling every mystery that comes along. I can't help but worry about you."

"Relax, Mom," Robin said, planting a kiss on her mother's forehead. "Nothing's going to happen to me."

"Well, you'd better run along to bed now, dear. It's late and there's nothing you can do tonight to solve the problem, so try to get to sleep."

"I can't even solve my math problems tonight," Robin laughed. "Better call me early in the morning. I'll be fresh then and can whip through them in no time."

4.

Rancho Lucia

THE FOLLOWING day after school Robin and Mindy met, as they had arranged, in the school parking lot where Michael had left the Heap. Since they were not in the same homeroom, this was the first time they had seen each other since the previous night.

"Is Kevin coming down to the ranch, too?" Mindy asked as they got into the car to wait for Michael.

"You know that nothing would keep him away except football, and team tryouts are this afternoon. He and Joe and umpteen other boys are dying to make the team and have a chance to do or die for dear old Pacific Point."

"Well, Kevin's certain," Mindy said. "He's got brains, brawn, *and* experience from junior high days, but I don't know about Joe."

"He's sure got the build for it," Robin said, "and he's smart, but I'll bet he's never played football in his life. It's jolly old cricket and soccer in England, you know."

"Or something called Rugby," Mindy laughed. "Maybe he'll make the second team, anyway."

"Hey, did you bring the box the fish was in?" Robin suddenly broke in, looking quickly around to the rear seat of the station wagon.

"No, we used our heads for once in our lives—or, rather, Michael used *his* head. He felt it might be safer to leave it home until after school. We'll swing around and pick it up on the way to the ranch."

It wasn't long before they saw tall, good-looking Michael running toward the car, and Robin felt her heart beat a little faster at his approach. He was too slightly built for football, but he had been elected captain of the track team last year, and he had skippered his yacht, "Stormalong," to the Club championship at Monteleone the previous summer.

There's no one quite like Mike, Robin thought to herself.

"Hi, you two!" he greeted them, tossing a couple of candy bars in their laps. "Here's something to keep you from starving until we get to the ranch and Mamacita's dinner."

"Thanks a million!" Robin said with pretended sarcasm. "You *would* spoil my good resolution to get rid of a few excess pounds, wouldn't you?"

"Excess pounds!" Michael exclaimed. "Why, Robin, I think you look just great the way you are."

He settled himself in the driver's seat, fastened his seat belt, and stepped on the starter, not noticing the flush that colored Robin's cheeks. The motor failed to respond, however, and when his second attempt brought only the same grinding sound, he clicked open the belt and jumped out.

"Now what the dickens!" he muttered as he opened the hood. "It started all right this morning."

He looked under the car to be sure there was no leak, and then, still complaining under his breath, began to check the spark plugs and the wiring system.

"I wish I could help," Robin called out to him, "but what I don't know about cars would fill a book."

"Dames aren't supposed to know about engines, so relax," he laughed. "Anyway, I think I've found the trouble, and I have a sneaking suspicion I know who caused it. Take a look over there."

He pointed to a dilapidated old car which, with many chugs and puffs, was coming toward them.

"See if you don't catch a gleam in the eye of the owner of that piece of junk."

"It's Tony!" Mindy called out. "What did he do,

Mike? Don't tell me it's another of his practical jokes."

"It's a joke, all right, but not very practical," Michael said as he continued to work under the hood. "I guess he wanted to see how long it would take me to find out that he'd disconnected the distributor head. Wait till I catch up with him! I'll fix his wagon."

Michael laughed good-naturedly and shook his fist at the rapidly disappearing car.

It didn't take him long to get the Heap going again, and in a few minutes they were at the Hunters' house. The old Japanese gardener, setting out some gay red petunias along the curb of the driveway, waved as they drove by. Manuela was waiting for them at the top of the wide steps, a beautiful Spanish shawl draped loosely around her shoulders against the wind blowing in from the beach. Her thick black hair, still untouched by gray, was piled high on her head and held in place by a large but delicately fashioned tortoise-shell comb.

"Robin Kane! *Querida mia!*" she called out as she ran gracefully down the stone steps to the car. *"Bienvenida,* welcome, *senorita!"*

"Gracias, Manuela," Robin replied warmly. She was impressed as always by the gracious manner of this lady who, only two years ago, had been mistress of the vast and once prosperous Rancho Lucia.

Dona Manuela Avila, the last of a distinguished Spanish family, had been forced to give up her ranch after a series of droughts had depleted the herd of

cattle and ruined the crops. The decision to sell the
ancestral home had been a heartbreaking one for her.
Despite her financial need, she had refused several
good offers because she felt the prospective buyers
didn't really appreciate the lovely old adobe house
and its handsome furnishings. But then Mr. Hunter
had come along, and their meeting had proved mu-
tually advantageous. Manuela had accepted his offer
to become his housekeeper and care for Mindy and
Michael at their home in Pacific Point. Mr. Hunter,
in turn, found the peace and beauty of Rancho Lucia
a welcome escape from the demands of his work, and
a perfect vacation spot for his children and their
friends.

Manuela always said, after visiting the ranch, that
it was just like going home again. Old Mamacita,
who had been with her for years, had stayed on after
Mr. Hunter bought the place. Her husband, easygoing
José, continued to manage the ranch. Here, however,
Mindy's father had made many innovations. The once
scanty herd had been replaced by prize Hereford cattle; the bunkhouse where the cowhands lived had been
enlarged and renovated; and the corral fences had
been mended. Mr. Hunter had even replanted the old
vineyards with new hardy grapes he had imported
from Portugal.

Although Manuela still loved the ranch, she now
had no regrets about selling it. Her days were full
overseeing the housekeeping details, planning the

meals, and making sure that the gardens and lawns were kept in perfect order.

As Michael went into the house to get the box, Manuela leaned on the edge of the car window, seemingly eager to talk to the two girls.

"You know, my dear, ever since last night when Michael and Mindy tell me about the golden fish, I think about it. So sad such a beautiful thing is lost! Then this afternoon, while I take the siesta, there comes to me a story my grandfather, Don Eduardo, tell me long, long ago."

"About the fish?" Robin asked eagerly.

"I like to believe it was about the same fish that is lost," Manuela answered softly. "You have seen the wreck of the big Spanish ship down at Breakwater, no?"

"Oh, yes. Robin and I have ridden our ponies up to the top of the cliff and looked down at it many times," Mindy said.

"And dreamed about all the treasure there may be in her hold!" Robin added.

"No treasure, I'm afraid," the old lady sighed, "only legends. Years ago when that ship hit the rocks and sank, the brothers of San Andrea's Mission and some fishermen risked their lives to rescue the men on board. That I always knew. Everyone has heard of their bravery, but only a few old ones like myself know about the fish."

"Yes, go on, Manuela," Robin urged gently.

"When the captain of the ill-fated ship finally made his way back to Spain, he sent a beautiful gold fish as a thank offering to be put in the mission chapel, and some money, too."

"What's that about money?" Michael asked, coming back just in time to catch the end of the sentence.

Robin quickly repeated what Manuela had told them, adding, "I wonder why in the world he sent a fish?"

"Ah, you young people," Manuela laughed, shaking her finger at them. "You do not study the saints as we did when I was a little girl. You see, San Andrea is the patron saint of fishermen. He it is who intercedes for them that they should have full nets. So, the good captain sent a fish of gold for the chapel, and pieces of gold for the fishermen." She stretched out her hands in a gesture of generosity.

"But what happened to the fish and the mission?" Robin asked. "The old chapel at Breakwater looks as if it has been deserted for years."

"That is so," Manuela said sadly. "The Spanish captains found landing there to be too treacherous— too many ships met disaster—so they sailed to other ports. For a time the fishermen stayed on; then they, too, drifted away. So eventually the good brothers moved the mission back into the hill country."

"And did they take the fish with them?" Robin asked.

"Who knows?" Manuela replied with a slight shrug

of her shoulders. "Perhaps Mindy's father? Ask him where they found San Andrea's fish. He may know. Now on your way, and be careful! Now I worry about you *and* the fish!"

As soon as they were out of the driveway, Robin reached for the box which Michael had put on the rear seat.

"I want to look at those newspapers," she said as she untied the string.

"Why, Robin, they were all torn to bits. You won't be able to read them," Mindy said. "Besides, since when have *you* become so interested in current events?"

"Use your head, Mindy!" Robin snapped. "It isn't news I'm after. It's evidence. Maybe I can find out where this paper came from. If it's not a local one we may have a lead."

As she talked she had been poking around through the torn paper, occasionally pulling out a piece and handing it to Mindy, who smoothed it out and spread it on her lap.

"Now, do all these bits and pieces have anything in common?" Robin asked excitedly. "Do they make any sense to you?"

"Well," Mindy said slowly, studying them carefully, "they look as though they might be part of a headline."

"Righto!" Robin exclaimed. "Now let's see if we can figure out what paper they're from."

"Oh, you two!" Michael laughed as he skillfully maneuvered the car through the increasingly heavy traffic. "It's probably last week's *Chronicle,* and if you look hard enough you'll come up with the 'Family Scene,' too."

"Darn it, you're right," Robin groaned, pulling some additional pieces from the box. "Here's old Fatso's head! I'd recognize me anywhere! There goes another lead blasted to bits."

"Don't take it so hard, Robin, old girl," Michael said. "Something's bound to turn up to give us a clue. It always has, you know."

"I keep telling myself that," Robin replied. "When Nugget disappeared, we had the sign of the blue pelican, but in this case we have absolutely nothing to go on."

The three fell silent for a time. Each was trying hard to piece together the little they knew. But when they turned off on the road leading through the Santa Lucia Mountains and the San Antonio River Valley, conversation began to buzz again.

This was the country they all loved. The green grazing lands were dotted with willow and cottonwood trees, with here and there a lazy stream winding down the gentle slopes from the dark mountains in the distance.

"Isn't it the most beautiful place in the whole world?" Mindy exclaimed as the weathered corral fence of Rancho Lucia came into view.

"Especially now that Nugget is back," Robin agreed. "It would never have been the same if we hadn't found him."

They hadn't gone far inside the gate before they caught sight of Mr. Hunter waving to them from the front porch. Even from a distance Robin's first impression was that he looked tired. His shoulders were stooped, and as he came out to meet them his stride wasn't as lively as usual. Michael, always sensitive to his father's changing moods, must have noticed it, too.

"Gee, Dad looks beat. I wonder if anything new has come up," he mused.

As the station wagon rolled to a halt, Felipe, Mamacita's little grandson, came running from the back of the house. His black eyes were shining.

"Hey! *Amigos!* Where is my friend Amy?" he called out, disappointment clouding his face when he failed to see her in the car. "I have some baby kittens to show her, out in the stable."

"Oh, she'll be awfully disappointed, Felipe," Robin said, getting out of the car, grabbing up the little boy, and swinging him around. "She had a dancing lesson today, so she couldn't come. She'll be down soon, though, especially when she hears about the kittens you have."

"Now, be a good boy and run and tell Mamacita we're here and starving as usual," Mindy said, anxious to be free to talk with her father.

Felipe ran off, followed by Perro, the big shepherd dog who, when he wasn't out on the range with the *vaqueros,* was the constant companion of the little boy.

"How is my family?" Mr. Hunter asked, embracing Mindy with one arm and Robin with the other. "I know that finding the box in the Heap must have upset you as much as it did me, especially since—"

He cut the sentence short and turned his attention to Michael, who was just behind the girls, the box under his arm.

Robin immediately caught the implication that all might not be going well with the picture.

"Nothing more has happened on the set, has it?" she asked him, concern in her voice.

"I guess I should have known I couldn't hide anything from you, Robin," Mr. Hunter answered, smiling down at her upturned face. "Yes, several things have happened. I can't for the life of me figure out why we should be running into so many snags."

"Golly, I'm sorry to hear that, Dad," Michael said soberly.

Their conversation was interrupted as Mamacita, wearing a gaily colored full skirt and bright blouse, came to the door and rang the dinner bell.

"Let's go in and you can tell us what's been going on while we're eating," Mindy suggested, putting her arm affectionately around her father. "Maybe we can give you some help."

"A good idea, honey," Mr. Hunter replied, his mood brightening.

"And who knows?" Michael said. "Maybe Robin can help you out of your dilemma."

5.

THE WARM late-day air was filled with the spicy aroma of Mamacita's cooking mingled with the scent of the rose geraniums and verbena which grew in wild profusion around the sprawling veranda. As the Hunters and Robin turned to enter the house they caught sight of the setting sun, making a last burst of brilliant color in the western sky. A peaceful quiet had settled over the ranch, the stillness broken only by the far-off sound of a *vaquero* strumming a guitar in the bunkhouse. Coming in from the bright light, Robin and the others needed a minute or two to become accustomed to the dimness of the living room. Like many ranch houses, this one had been built with thick adobe walls and small windows to keep out the heat. Deep green tile floors and white walls added to the cool atmosphere of the spacious room, where generations of Avilas had gathered in former years.

"Old *Señor* Carlos looks pleased to have us back," Mindy said, looking up at a painting of a handsome, dark-eyed old gentleman.

"He's apparently the only one of Manuela's ancestors who had a sense of humor," Michael remarked, glancing around at the austere family portraits in their heavy frames. "The rest look cross as bears. Even the women."

"I'll bet they weren't actually that unpleasant," Robin commented as they went in for dinner. "I've seen Manuela look like a thundercloud when we've done something she didn't like, and the next minute she would be all smiles."

"She's really an angel," Mr. Hunter said slowly as they sat down at the table, "and I don't know what in the world we'd all do without her."

"You talk about me? No?" Mamacita exclaimed, appearing at that moment from the kitchen with an enormous steaming dish.

"Yes, you're an angel, too, Mamacita," Mr. Hunter said with a warm smile. "What have you concocted for us tonight?"

"Beans, tonight, only beans, *señor*," Mamacita said in a mournful voice, at the same time giving a surreptitious wink in the direction of Robin and Mindy. She placed the dish in front of Mr. Hunter, then stood back of his chair, her hands on her ample hips, her shoulders shaking with suppressed laughter.

"Beans, indeed!" he exclaimed, leaning over to inhale the delicious smell. "It's chicken *molé!* My favorite dish, and no one does it better than you, Mamacita. Always just the right amount of chocolate. *Gracias, señora!*"

"Chocolate and chicken!" Robin exclaimed. "What a funny combination, but I must say it smells divine."

"It *is* divine," Mindy said. "But the chocolate isn't the sweet kind, like candy bars. It is more like a spice. They grind up the whole chocolate beans, and the flavor is just out of this world."

"It is said that Montezuma, the last Aztec emperor, treated the Spanish conquistadors to turkey with *molé* sauce," Mr. Hunter told them.

"And ended up being captured by Cortes!" Michael laughed. "Fine reward for serving them such a delicacy!"

"You ought to ask your mother to try the recipe," Mindy said to Robin, "although no two people agree on the ingredients—except the chocolate!"

"I guess we keep her so busy with hamburgers and things we can cook out on the grill that she doesn't have a chance to experiment," Robin laughed.

"But after the meal we had last night at your house, you can't say she doesn't sling a mean chili con carne," Michael said, "to say nothing about her cherry pies!"

Robin was glad to see Mr. Hunter's mood lighten as he served them. She wondered to herself if perhaps the things he had been worrying about might be unimportant after all—just little annoyances that can be aggravating to a busy man. Then she remembered that the theft of the fish was not a little thing.

The four of them chatted for a time about the ranch, about some new palomino horses Mr. Hunter had ordered, and about how difficult it was to get experienced hands to take care of the stock.

"I've often wondered how palominos got their name," Mindy said. "Is it Spanish?"

"Oh, I know!" Robin piped up. "I looked it up right after your father gave me Nugget. *Palomillo* is the Spanish diminutive of *la paloma,* which means pigeon or dove. *Palomillo* means little dove. The word was used to designate horses like Nugget, which are brownish-gray or gold in color, like a dove. In time it became Americanized to palomino."

"I didn't know that myself," Mr. Hunter remarked. "Good for you, Robin!"

Robin, who had been anxious to find out more about the fish, changed the subject abruptly. "Mr. Hunter," she said, "is the lost fish the same one the Spanish captain gave to the mission years ago? This afternoon we heard a story about just such a fish."

"I believe it's the same one," he replied. "One of Westpark's researchers dug up the legend and finally traced the fish to the museum. There isn't much doubt about its being San Andrea's fish."

"What does a researcher do, Daddy?" Mindy asked.

"I'm glad you asked, honey," her father answered. "It always pleases me when people ask about a word or a phrase they don't understand. It shows a lively mind. When we make a movie or a television feature, we want to be sure that every aspect of the production is correct—the costumes, the background, and the story itself. So every studio employs people who do nothing but check on such details for authenticity."

"Oh, I'd love a job like that," Mindy said. "Now go on about the fish. How did it get from the mission to the museum?"

"Yes, why didn't the brothers take San Andrea's fish with them when they left Breakwater?" Robin asked.

"No one seems to know why, Robin," Mr. Hunter replied. "All the information the museum had was that it was purchased from a reputable art dealer several years ago."

"And what did *he* say about it?" Robin asked eagerly.

"Only that he had bought it at an auction of art objects, along with a lot of other church furnishings such as candlesticks, altar vases, and statues. Unfortunately the origins of many beautiful works of art become obscured over the years. The San Andrea brothers themselves may have lost sight of why the fish was given to the mission in the first place."

"Maybe they had to sell it to get money for something they needed very badly," Robin said thoughtfully.

After Mamacita had cleared the table and brought in a dish of plump figs and a large bowl of whipped cream for dessert, Mr. Hunter sat back in his chair.

"Well, Michael," he said, "we might as well get to the rather unpleasant subject of the film. You may be right about Robin. She's shown in the past that she's a pretty good detective. Perhaps she can make some sense out of the latest happenings."

"Don't forget I had Mindy and Michael and my brother to help me," Robin said with a smile. "I've made them bona fide members of my agency!"

"Now go on and tell us what happened," Mindy urged her father. "We're dying of curiosity."

"Well, the disappearance of the fish was bad enough," Mr. Hunter began. "It meant that I had to revise the shooting schedule so that some scenes in which the fish wasn't used could be shot first. I worked that out and gave instructions for the commentator of the series, Waldo Stern, to be on location early Monday morning at Breakwater." He stopped, as if puzzling over the matter.

"Yes, yes, go on," Robin said, impatient to hear the whole story.

"Monday morning came and no Waldo!" Mr. Hunter said.

"Where was he?" "What happened?" "He didn't quit, did he?" They were all asking questions at once.

"No, he's completely reliable. He didn't quit," Mr. Hunter continued. "When mid-morning came and he hadn't appeared, I called his home only to learn that he had left for the Westpark Films studio in Los Angeles the night before!"

"Los Angeles!" Mindy exclaimed. "Why did he go there?"

"When I finally tracked him down, he told me a woman had phoned him, supposedly on orders from me, telling him to report there for some special-effect shots at eleven the next morning. He was as puzzled as I was when he found I'd never issued such an order. He was about to call *me* to see what was going on."

"Did anyone at Breakwater know anything about the call?" Michael asked.

"No one, so far as I could find out by doing some discreet questioning."

"Even if they did, they probably wouldn't admit it," Robin reasoned, half to herself.

"How long did it take Mr. Stern to get back to Breakwater?" Mindy asked.

"Oh, he returned immediately and was all set to go on this morning when, boom, we had a power failure!" Mr. Hunter threw up his hands in a gesture of despair.

"What rotten luck," Michael said. "That meant another delay, I suppose."

"The electricians worked most of the day trying to track down the trouble." Mr. Hunter sighed. "They were sure it was somewhere on the set. Then some bright young man suggested what should have been obvious in the beginning, I suppose—that they check the wires coming into the set from the municipal poles."

"And that's where the trouble was," Robin declared positively. "Someone had tampered with the wires."

"Robin, you're way ahead of me!" Mr. Hunter said, leaning over and giving her a pat on the head.

"Well, as you were talking I was thinking about the fish and the phony phone call and now this," Robin said, toying with her spoon, "and it occurred to me that someone must be trying to sabotage the film."

"I'm interested that you, too, should think of sabotage as a possibility, Robin," Mr. Hunter said, slowly turning the stem of his goblet as he spoke. "I had considered that possibility, but then I couldn't for the life of me think who could benefit by that kind of trick."

"That's what we have to find out," Robin replied, convinced that her theory was right.

"Well, it *could* be," Mr. Hunter admitted. "The power cable *was* found to be badly frayed, and it's possible that someone cut it deliberately so there would be a blackout when the high-powered spot-lights were turned on. We all assumed it was just an accident."

"How did the people on the set react?" Michael asked his father.

"I think the general feeling was one of frustration more than anything else," Mr. Hunter said. "The electricians and grips have worked with me before, and I know they pride themselves on doing a good job. The extras, of course, didn't mind the delay, because they are paid by the day, and it meant they'd get a fatter paycheck."

"Wait a minute, Daddy!" Mindy spoke up. "If the extras get more pay when there's a delay, what's to stop one of them from trying deliberately to slow things up?"

"You've got a point there, Mindy," Robin said, "except for one little detail. Mr. Hunter, did anyone hear you phone Mindy Monday night?"

"No, I was in the office alone. I remember distinctly because I had been working on the shooting schedule after everyone else had left the set for the day."

"Then how would an extra know where Mindy and Michael were that night, and how could the box get into the Heap a little more than an hour after you called my house?"

"I don't know, Robin," Mr. Hunter sighed. "This whole thing has assumed such a mysterious aspect. I'm as puzzled as you all are."

"Can you think of anything we can do to help you, Daddy?" Mindy asked. She got up from the table and went around to sit on the arm of her father's chair.

"Not at the moment," he answered. "Seeing all of you and talking over this whole thing has helped a lot. I intend to be on the alert for any further attempts to throw a monkey wrench into the project."

"I've got an idea!" Robin suddenly cried, snapping her fingers. "We're just not going to *let* things go on happening. We're going to *make* them happen! We're going to trap this mysterious Phantom!"

"Phantom!" Mindy exclaimed. "Robin, what on earth do you mean?"

"That's the way I picture him," Robin said slowly, the tip of her index finger placed dramatically against her lips, "a mysterious someone, bent on harassing Mr. Hunter. Now if we could just—" She stopped.

"Just what, Robin? Go on!" Mindy was impatient.

"Hold it, Min," Michael said. "Give her a chance to think. What's your plan, Robin?"

"Well, I'll have to work out the details, of course," Robin said, "but if we could create a situation which the Phantom might see as another opportunity to cause trouble, we *could* trap him! Like the spider inviting the fly into his parlor."

"That's an interesting possibility, my dear," Mr. Hunter said, "although it would take a bit of doing. Why don't you all put your heads together and see if you can come up with a plan? I'm willing to give it a try as long as you don't put yourselves in any danger."

"I think it's a swell idea!" Michael said. "Let's work out something on the way home tonight. Let's remember, though, to keep this whole thing under our collective hat!"

"We'll want to tell Kevin," Mindy said. "He's sure to have some ideas of his own."

"Natch! Kevin is family!" Michael laughed.

"I take it you're not going to spend the night down here?" Mr. Hunter said.

During the summer the young people spent a good deal of their time at Rancho Lucia. They all enjoyed the casualness of the life, with indulgent Mamacita cooking her savory dishes for them, the pack trips to the nearby mountains, the lazy days and cool evenings. Now the beginning of school and all the activities in Pacific Point had somewhat curtailed their trips.

"No, we're going back tonight," Michael replied in answer to his father's question. "Kev would be furious if we stayed down here without him, and besides, day after tomorrow is a school holiday, and I mean to get caught up on all my work so I can enjoy it."

"Yipes! I'd almost forgotten!" Mindy cried. "The teachers have to go to a convention. Hurrah for our side! Let's do something real special!"

"How would you like to go scuba diving?" Michael

suggested with an air of deliberate casualness.

"Scuba diving!" Mindy exclaimed. "Don't be silly, Mike. You know none of us know the first thing about skin diving."

"Besides, you need all kinds of equipment—special suits, flippers, and stuff," Robin added, "but wouldn't I love to try it!" Her eyes began to shine at the thought of a new sport.

"Maybe *we* don't have the gear, but I know someone who has," Michael said, obviously enjoying teasing the two girls.

"Mike, you don't! Who?" Robin went over and beat her fists on Michael's shoulders.

"I was going to surprise you," Michael said, pretending to crumple under Robin's attack. "Spare me, kind lady, and I'll tell you. Yesterday Joe and I got to talking about surfing on our way to history class. He said he's never had a chance to try it, but last summer he went to Norway on a vacation and took scuba lessons."

"Jiminy, that's great!" Robin exclaimed. "I've never seen anyone skin dive in my whole life."

"Don't tell me Pacific Point has been missing something," Mr. Hunter laughed. "Who is this Joe you're talking about?"

They told him about their new friend and how easily he had fitted into their group.

"We haven't met his uncle yet," Robin said. "He's writing a book and is very busy, but Mom's going to invite him over for a cookout as soon as Daddy gets back from San Francisco."

"Go on, Mike, tell us more about Joe. Is he really a good diver?" Mindy asked.

"Well, he didn't come right out and *say* he was an expert," Michael replied. "You know Joe. But it seems he spent the whole summer at it and got such a bang out of it that he bought himself an outfit and had it sent here when he came to the States. As a matter of fact, that's why he had to hitchhike from New York—he spent part of his travel money on the equipment."

"I'm dying to try it, too," Mindy said. "Do you think he'll let us use his suit and stuff?"

"I was coming to that," her brother replied. "There's just one hitch. It seems the first rule of scuba diving is that you never go in alone, at least not until you're a real pro and then only in an actual emergency."

"Oh, drat it!" Mindy said impatiently. "Isn't there anyone we know who has a suit?"

"I can't think of a soul," Robin said. She had already mentally checked over her friends and acquaintances. "Surfing and water-skiing have always been the rage around here, and I guess no one thought about skin diving."

"I suppose we'll have to sit on the sidelines and watch Joe, then." Mindy's voice was petulant. "But I doubt if we'll be able to see very much with him on the bottom of Monteleone Bay!"

"Now, Mindy, dear," Mr. Hunter said, "don't despair so easily. I might be able to get hold of some suits and have them sent up in time for your outing."

Mindy was immediately all smiles. She gave her father an appreciative hug and then, looking at Robin, exclaimed, "Aren't we lucky? Isn't Daddy the greatest?"

Robin was delighted, too. She thanked Mr. Hunter profusely, but at the same time she wondered, as she sometimes had before, if his eagerness to fill Mindy's every wish was altogether wise.

6.

Robin's Plan

"I'VE JUST got to see Nugget before I leave," Robin said. "Even if there isn't time for a ride, I can at least give him a lump of sugar."

They headed for the stable where the beautiful palomino and the other horses were kept. Robin broke into a run in her eagerness to see her beloved pet again. Matt, whom Mr. Hunter had put in special charge of Nugget and his stablemates, had seen them coming and was waiting for them in front of the barn. Robin couldn't help but notice how different his appearance was from that of the haunted, frightened man she had encountered in the hills with El Gato. Matt's small son, Jeff, close on his father's heels, held up one of the new kittens that little Felipe had mentioned.

Matt touched the brim of his cap as he greeted them.

"I'm glad to see you, young lady," he said to Robin. "Nugget must have missed you these last few days. He's been as restless as a mother hen who's lost a chick. Won't even let me curry him without kicking up a fuss. You go talk to him. You can straighten him out, all right!"

"Oh, Nugget!" Robin called out as she hurried past the stalls where Sutter's Gold, Lucky, and Sunshine were quietly eating their oats.

The beautiful horse must have heard her, for he began to whinny and paw the floor impatiently. As she came into sight, he tossed his head up and down in obvious joy, his shining golden mane waving from side to side. When Robin put out her closed hand, he nuzzled it with his moist nose to find the sugar which he knew it held. Robin unlatched the leather thong on the low door and went inside. She stroked the smoothly curried coat of the horse Mr. Hunter had given her for her very own. Nugget quieted as she continued to croon softly into his ear.

"I'll be back next weekend and we'll go for a long ride, Nugget," she whispered. "Nugget, dear Nugget, do you hear?"

"Of course he hears," Mindy said, watching Nugget nod his head as Robin had trained him to do. "I do believe that horse understands everything you say to him. I wish my Lucky could do tricks, too."

Robin noticed a hint of acerbity in her friend's voice. It was sometimes hard for Mindy not to show a little jealousy over other people's accomplishments. Her father's tendency to overindulge her had the effect of making Mindy think that everything came without much effort on her part.

It's just like her tennis game, Robin thought to herself. *But it isn't entirely her fault. She's getting more self-reliant all the time, but she still needs a little help.*

She curbed her momentary impatience with her dearest friend. As she came out of the stall she said, "Why, Mindy, you could teach Lucky to do anything you want, if you'd just try."

"I suppose so," Mindy conceded. She picked up one of the fluffy gray kittens that had wandered into the stable and held it gently against her cheek. "I'm too impatient, I guess—but just wait till next summer! I'll have Lucky jumping through a flaming hoop, just like in the circus!"

She was smiling again as they left the stable and said good-bye to Matt and Jeff.

"We're planning a pack trip for a new friend of ours," she told Matt, "so please get an extra saddle ready."

"*And* another horse," Robin laughed. "A saddle

without a horse wouldn't do us much good."

"The new palominos should be here in a few days. I'll have the pick of the lot ready for you," Matt assured them.

Walking past the house on the way to the Heap, where Michael was waiting for them, they saw Mamacita on the veranda, her head nodding. Felipe was fast asleep on her lap. She roused herself at the sound of their footsteps, blew them many kisses from the tips of her pudgy fingers, and then waved until they were out of sight.

They had no sooner gotten in the car than Michael brought up the subject of Robin's proposal.

"Now about that plan of yours, Robin—where did you figure on setting up the trap?" he asked.

"Yes, and exactly what kind of trap did you have in mind?" Mindy added.

"Oh, jeepers," Robin said. "It seemed like a swell idea when I thought of it at dinner time, but now I'm not so sure. Where do I get these wild ideas?"

"Take it easy, old girl," Michael said, knowing from experience there was usually a sound basis behind Robin's sometimes sudden impulses. "I'll bet you can work it out. Let's try approaching the problem from a scientific point of view."

"Oh, Mike, you know Robin and I aren't any good at science!" Mindy said. "If you and Kev hadn't helped us last year we might never have passed our final examinations."

"Maybe he just means for us to analyze the situation," Robin said. "Right, Mike?"

"That's the idea. Then maybe we can come up with some helpful deductions."

"You sound just like Sherlock Holmes," Mindy laughed, "but let's give it a try. You begin, Robin."

"Well, first of all, we can be sure our Phantom knows his way around the movie set and is familiar enough with the picture to realize the importance of San Andrea's fish."

"Yes, and we can assume he has *some* information about our family," Mindy said, "or he wouldn't have put the box in the Heap."

"I figure the Phantom must have a car," Robin said, "or he couldn't have traveled from Breakwater to Pacific Point so fast after your father phoned last night."

"We're calling him the Phantom," Michael mused, "but come to think of it, we don't know whether our suspect is male or female. Remember, Mr. Stern told Dad it was a woman who called his house to give him the false instructions."

"Actually that doesn't prove anything, Mike," Robin said. "The Phantom could have disguised his voice or simply had some woman make the call for him. I can't quite picture a woman climbing an electric pole and cutting the wires, can you?"

"Well, with everyone screaming about equal rights for women these days, you can't be too sure!" Michael chuckled. "I can imagine you doing it, Robin," he added mischievously.

"How about the trap you're thinking of setting?" Mindy asked. "Would it be in Breakwater or Pacific Point?"

"I haven't thought that out, either," Robin replied, "but I have a hunch it would be easier to do at home. There wouldn't be as many complications there as there would be in Breakwater."

No one said anything for a while, each silently trying to invent a situation that would entice the Phantom into further action.

"The trouble with trying to do anything off the set is that it wouldn't have anything to do with Daddy's film," Mindy finally said, "and that's what the Phantom obviously wants to ruin."

"Hey, you've given me an idea!" Robin cried, grabbing Mindy's arm. "If only your father will go along with it!"

"Listen, Robin," Michael said, "you know Dad will help any way he can. What's the inspiration?"

"Well, you know at the beginning of any picture, in addition to the title, they always list everybody who worked on the film who gets credit—the director, the producer, the scriptwriter, the costume designer, and so forth and so on. And behind all these credits on the screen, and the title, they sometimes have a drawing or a painting or just a decoration that is—is characteristic of the story."

"Yes, yes, we know what you mean," Mindy said, impatient to hear the plan. "Daddy calls that part of the film the main title. They consider it very important. But go on, Robin."

"Those credits have to have some kind of background," Robin repeated, as if she had not heard her friend.

"Okay, okay, okay!" Mindy's voice was sharp now. "You've said all that and we *know* about main titles! What's the plan?"

"Well," Robin said imperturbably, "let's suppose your father decided to use a drawing for his background. And suppose he wanted to give the film some extra publicity. Therefore, why couldn't he have competition for the best piece of art which was submitted?"

"He could, but how would that trap the Phantom?" Mindy asked. "I don't get what you are driving at, my dearest friend."

"I know I'm not making myself clear," Robin admitted. "I'm just sort of thinking out loud. . . . But to go on, why couldn't the competition be publicized all over, so no one could miss it? It could be announced at our school, in the local paper, and on the set in Breakwater."

"All right," Mike said a little dubiously, *"then* what happens?"

"Then," Robin said eagerly, "the best of the submissions are weeded out, the winner is announced, and the prizewinning drawing is prominently displayed for all to admire!"

"Oh, Robin," Michael exclaimed. "What a perfectly terrific idea! The prizewinner is displayed—and enter the Phantom!"

"To destroy it or to steal it!" Mindy cried, clapping her hands in excitement.

"Exactly!" Robin echoed her excitement. "Everything he's done up to now has been something to slow down the picture. Someone, for some reason we can't even guess at, doesn't want your father to complete the picture."

"Or," Michael said gloomily, "someone wants to cost Dad a lot of money!"

"I know, Michael," Robin said softly, "but this time we will be ready for him. When he tries to get at the prizewinner, we will spring our little trap. We're sure to catch him."

"Robin, Robin!" Michael said admiringly. "What an imagination! It will work. I'm sure it will work perfectly, just because the Phantom will think it will be easy to break in. Where will we set the trap? It will have to be someplace that we are familiar with."

"You're right, Michael," Robin agreed. "The Municipal Art Gallery is too big, and so is the school auditorium. We would have trouble spinning our web in either of those big old barns."

"How about your father's studio?" Mindy suggested eagerly.

"Mindy, you're a genius!" Robin exclaimed. "There it is, right under my nose, and I never thought of it!"

"You're right, Sis," Michael agreed. "It's not too big, it's right here in town, and it's where we can keep an eye on it. Now, Robin, one more question. How do you intend to spin this web you keep talking about?"

"That's where you and Kevin will have to help," Robin said. "It'll take you two to rig up some electrical gadgets. Mindy and I would be useless at that sort of thing. You boys know so much more about electronics than we do."

"Come on, Robin," Michael chuckled, "no need to flatter us. I'm sure Kev will be as anxious to help as I am. What's the plan? You know we're always ready to help you."

"Well, if we could install some kind of electric buzzer that would sound off inside our house if anyone tried to get into the studio after the exhibition, we might nab the culprit!" Robin announced eagerly. "We could make a great show of going off somewhere, to the Club or your house, so the Phantom would think our place was deserted, then I'd sneak back and wait for him to sneak into the studio and set off the buzzer."

"It's a great idea, except for one thing," Michael said soberly. "Don't think for one minute, old girl, that you're going to hide out in the house by yourself. That should be *my* detail."

"He's right, Robin," Mindy said. "We don't know how dangerous the Phantom may be. He might even have a gun or a knife or something! I'm afraid of what might happen."

"I hadn't thought of that," Robin confessed. "I guess I will need some help." She smiled warmly at Mike. "You're elected."

"We'll call Daddy the first thing when we get home," Mindy said, "and see if he'll go along with the plan. Then tomorrow we can put the announcement of the competition on the bulletin boards at school. The free day this week will give people extra time to work on it."

"Wonderful," Robin said, "and if Daddy's home I'll ask him if we can use his studio. I'm sure it will be all right with him. He might even give us a hand in getting ready for the show."

"Ooooh! I can't wait!" Mindy cried. "If it only works!"

By now they were approaching Robin's house. As they passed the old Williams place—the Haunted House—Michael asked, "Do you think we should let Joe in on the plan?"

"Jiminy!" Mindy said. "Joe's been swell, but we don't know him awfully well. All we know is what he's told us. We can't be sure whether he can keep a secret or not."

"As much as I like Joe, I don't think we should take any chances with this scheme," Robin said. "It's

too important to your father. Let's keep it to our-
selves."

Mindy and her brother agreed, and plans were
made for meeting the next day to work out the details
after Mr. Hunter and Mr. Kane had been consulted.

7.

The Phantom

AFTER BIDDING Mindy and Michael good night, Robin ran up the driveway toward her house. Light from the softly shaded lamps in the living room shone out on the patio. Catching a glimpse of her father through the window, seated in his favorite chair with his pipe and newspaper, she felt a warm glow flood over her. The happenings of the last two days had made her more apprehensive than she cared to admit, even to herself. With her father home, everything seemed somehow more secure. She ran into the house and impulsively threw herself into his lap as she used to do when she was a little girl.

"Oh, Daddy, I'm *so* glad you're back!" she exclaimed, unexpected tears welling up in her eyes. "You've been gone ages and ages."

"I'm glad to be home, honey," Mr. Kane answered, holding his daughter tightly, "but I've only been away a couple of days. To what do I owe this extraordinary welcome?"

He held her at arm's length and took a close look at her, sensing that something had upset her.

"Well, it *seems* like ages and ages," Robin laughed, brushing away a tear. "So much happened. Did Mom tell you about the fish?"

"Yes, dear, and I can understand your being worried about it, but you mustn't let it get you down. It's not like losing Nugget, and I'm pretty sure the fish will turn up in time."

"Oh, but it's not just the fish, Daddy," Robin cried, jumping up and looking through the door to the kitchen. "Where's Mom and Kevin? I want you all to hear what *else* has happened. It's awful!"

"Your mother's with Kevin in his room. It seems he's outgrown his school slacks again and Mother's seeing if they can be lengthened once more before they hit the ragbag."

"Come on, Daddy," Robin said, taking his hand, "let's go in there then."

"Hi, Sis!" Kevin called out as he heard her coming down the hall. "How's everything at the ranch?"

"Oh, everything's fine down there," Robin replied, "but you should hear what's been going on at Breakwater!"

"Hurry up and tell us, for pete's sake!" Kevin urged her. "Don't tell me the fish has turned up."

"No, not a word about the fish, but Mr. Hunter told us he's been bothered by phony telephone calls, and someone's been tampering with the electric lines so they've had a power failure, and I don't know what's going to happen next!"

Robin threw herself down on Kevin's bed.

"Does Mr. Hunter think these are deliberate attempts to harass him or Westpark Films?" Mr. Kane asked.

"It had occurred to him, I guess," Robin said. "When I mentioned that it sounded like sabotage to me, too, he felt even more strongly that there might be some one person behind all this. But he can't figure out who or why." Robin's usually bright face was clouded.

Mr. Kane sat down on Kevin's bed beside Robin.

"Now, Robin," he said softly, "you've got an imagination as big as Disneyland. Are you sure you're not exaggerating things?"

"Well, maybe," Robin conceded, "but if one more thing happens, I'll *know* it's not my imagination."

"You can't say it was her imagination in the case of the blue pelican, can you, Dad?" Kevin said in a burst of loyalty to his sister.

"Anyway, I've got a plan to catch the culprit if there *is* a culprit!" Robin said emphatically. "We worked it out on the way home from Rancho Lucia."

"Great!" Kevin cried. "Let's hear about it."

Before Robin had a chance to explain the trap, the brass bell which hung at the entrance to the patio rang impatiently. It was Michael, and he fairly burst into the living room when Mr. Kane opened the door. His face was tense and pale.

"Sorry to disturb you this way, Mr. Kane, but while we were at the ranch someone apparently disconnected the phone at our house. Manuela is all upset, and I didn't know what to do except come back here and use your phone. Mindy stayed home to try to calm things down."

"You know it's no bother, Mike," Mr. Kane assured him. "Did you say you think someone disconnected the phone? It isn't just out of order?"

"No, the wire leading into the house looks as though it had been yanked out," he replied.

Mrs. Kane, Robin, and Kevin had come out into the living room when they heard Michael arrive. Robin hoped that this latest development would convince her parents that her fears were not just imaginary. It must be obvious now that *something* was going on. This was the fourth suspicious episode!

"You'd better phone your father right away," Robin said, knowing that Mr. Hunter would probably call to see if his children had reached home safely after

driving back from the ranch. "He may have been trying to get you."

She and Michael went into the hall, and Robin perched on the edge of the table as the call was put through. She was eager to talk to Mr. Hunter, too. Michael held the phone a little away from his ear so that she, too, could hear the conversation. It turned out that Mr. Hunter, after trying unsuccessfully to phone his home, had reported the failure to the phone company. They had promised to have a repairman there the first thing in the morning. Michael's father had not, of course, been aware that the phone might have been tampered with.

"Are you sure?" he asked incredulously after Michael had told him of the disconnected wire. "Did you look at it carefully?"

"Probably not as carefully as I might have," Michael answered. "You know the wire goes into the house way around on the side near the rose garden, and it was pretty dark, but I'll look again with a flashlight when I get back. Here's Robin. She wants to talk with you, Dad."

"Hi, Mr. Hunter!" Robin greeted him, trying not to let her concern sound in her voice. "Please try not to worry about things at this end. I'm going to ask Daddy to drive back with Michael to be sure everything's all right and to calm Manuela down a bit. You know how excited she gets when anything goes wrong."

After talking a while longer about the latest apparent attempt to harass Mr. Hunter and his family, Robin broached the subject of her plan to catch the elusive Phantom.

"I haven't had a chance to discuss it with Daddy yet," she explained when she had outlined the scheme, "but I'm sure he'll go along with it if you approve. Do you, Mr. Hunter?" She nervously twisted the cord of the phone around her finger in her eagerness to hear his reaction.

"Robin, you never cease to amaze me!" he said after a few seconds' deliberation. "It's a clever idea, and although I'm not sure it will work, it *is* worth a try. And, as you say, it will also serve to give some publicity to the TV series. Go ahead, my dear. You've got my okay."

"Oh, thanks, Mr. Hunter!" she cried, almost dropping the phone in her excitement. "We'll check with you about details tomorrow."

Michael was as pleased as Robin, and together they returned to the living room to tell the others about the project. Robin tried to be brief, knowing Michael was anxious to start back home. She saw her father glance once or twice at Mrs. Kane with what she and Kevin laughingly called their "yes or no" look. Mr. Kane took a long puff on his pipe when he had heard her proposal, and after what seemed like hours to her, he, too, agreed to the plan.

"The only thing that made me hesitate," he said, "is the possibility of your having to cope with someone potentially dangerous. I know two is company, and three's a crowd, but would you consider letting me stand watch with you?"

Michael's answer was immediate and sincere.

"It's *not* an intrusion, sir," he said. "We don't want to take any chances of this thing failing, and I for one would feel a lot better with you there."

Robin quickly agreed. "There's only one problem," she said, "and that's how all three of us can sneak back into the house without being seen."

"I know you can work out that detail, Robin," Michael assured her. "Just give it a little thought. Let's not worry about it right now."

"You're right, Mike," she said. "There *are* more important things to straighten out first."

Turning to her father, she asked if he would mind driving back with Michael.

"You must be a mind reader, honey," he laughed. "I was about to suggest just that, but I couldn't get a word in edgewise!"

"I'm sorry, Daddy," Robin replied contritely. "I was jabbering too much, as usual. May Kevin and I go along with you?"

Mrs. Kane glanced at her watch and then at her husband.

"It's quite late," she said with a slight frown, "but I know you, Robin. You'd never go to sleep until your father got home, so go ahead!"

"Oh, Mom, you're the greatest!" Robin cried.

"Now, Kev, go get your big flashlight. I want to have a look at that telephone wire, too."

"Okay, my little detective," her brother said with a chuckle. "I might give it the once-over myself."

The Hunter mansion was ablaze with lights as they drove up. Manuela had apparently turned on every light in the house. She and Mindy were waiting in the hall for Michael's return. When Mindy caught sight of the Kanes, she ran out and grabbed Robin's hand. Her own hands, Robin noticed, were unnaturally cold.

"Oh, I'm so glad you're here!" she cried. "I was scared to death with only Manuela in this big old house!"

"Only Manuela?" Michael repeated incredulously. "What happened to the cook and Annie?"

"*Mios Dios!*" Manuela replied dramatically. "They leave. Packed up their belongings and left. Didn't even wait for a taxicab to come for them."

"That's rather odd, isn't it?" Mr. Kane asked in a calm voice. "Why should a disconnected phone cause such a precipitate departure?"

Manuela, before answering, motioned for them to follow her into the living room. She drew the curtains across the windows and the French doors which opened onto the terrace, then moved up some chairs in a close little circle around the sofa.

"It was not just the telephone, *señor*," Manuela said almost in a whisper, glancing over her shoulder.

"I did not tell Michael and Mindy the whole story."

"What do you mean?" Michael asked anxiously. "What else happened?"

"Just at dusk, cook comes to me saying she hears strange noises outside," Manuela said. "I go with her back to the kitchen and listen. Nothing. I hear nothing. Then Annie comes running from the dining room where she was waxing the table. She had heard the strange sounds, too."

"What sort of sounds?" Robin asked.

"Moaning, like the wind," Manuela said. "That's what they tell me, but there was no wind tonight. No! They say it was a ghost trying to get into the house."

"And you heard nothing either time?" Mr. Kane asked gently.

"No," Manuela replied, "but I *see* something. I go out on the terrace just in time to see a form, in a great gray cape, running like the wind toward the ocean!"

"Oh, Manuela, what's happening?" Mindy buried her face in her hands and moved closer to Robin.

"Probably nothing serious," Mr. Kane said, trying to reassure the little group. "You know it could be someone with a misguided sense of humor trying to play a joke on the servants."

"Could it be Tony, Mike?" Robin asked, recalling how Tony loved to play practical jokes and how he had tampered with the Heap.

"I doubt it very much." Michael shook his head as he answered. "Tony plays jokes, yes, but I've never known him to be malicious. He wouldn't wreck the telephone, and why would he want to scare the servants? He doesn't even know them."

"Manuela, are you sure your imagination wasn't playing tricks on you?" Robin asked. "After Annie and the cook thought they heard strange sounds, naturally you were upset. Could the 'ghost' have been a shadow or a wisp of fog or something?"

"No, my child, nothing like that," Manuela said positively. "But it could have been a man, for always it stay on the ground, running fast, not flying through the air like a true ghost."

"We can soon tell what kind of a creature it was," Robin said, getting up and taking the flashlight from Kevin. "I'm going out and see if I can find any footprints."

"Robin, you're *not!*" Mindy cried, grabbing Robin's arm. "Please don't let her go out there alone, Mr. Kane!"

"Okay, we'll all come along with you, Robin," Mr. Kane said. "There's safety in numbers, you know."

"I don't want to go, but *more* I don't want to stay here alone!" Manuela moaned, wrapping her shawl tightly around her shoulders. As she went past a table on the way to the door she picked up a heavy brass candlestick and tucked it under her arm. "Just in case!" she said to herself.

"Now, in what direction did he go, Manuela?" Robin asked when they reached the terrace.

"That way. Over there toward the far corner." She pointed down the beach where the Hunter property ended in a low stone breakwater.

Robin turned on the flashlight and shined it on the steps leading down to the sand. Then she waved it back and forth in wide arcs as she slowly went forward.

"Hey, look!" she cried suddenly. "Here are some tracks, and big ones, too. What *are* they?"

Everyone gathered around to see what she had found.

"Holy cow!" Kevin exclaimed. "These look like bird tracks!"

"And what a bird!" Michael cried when he, too, had had a chance to look at the prints. "Those marks must be a foot long!"

Mr. Kane knelt down and examined them, tracing the strange outline with his finger. He rubbed his chin in disbelief.

"It beats me," he said. "The owner of those webbed feet must be as big as an ostrich! But ostriches don't have webbed feet. And besides, whoever heard of an ostrich in Pacific Point?"

"Maybe it's a creature from outer space," Kevin suggested facetiously, "or an escapee from the San Diego zoo."

"You're all way off the track," Robin said. "Do you know what those tracks are?"

"No! What?" they all asked in one breath.

"Our Phantom has very cleverly cut up a pair of swimming fins and wired them to make the tracks of a giant bird. It's just a fake!"

"You know, I think you're right, Robin," Michael said. He had been examining one of the more distinct footprints. "Look, here's a perfect impression. What do you know! Robin, you're dead right!"

"The Phantom probably figured the fins would disguise the real size and shape of his footprints or shoe prints," Robin mused.

"And they made him look so—not like a human being!" Manuela added. *"Muy horrendo*—dreadful!"

They traced the marks all the way to the jetty, but on the other side of it they found nothing but smooth sand. It was as though the creature had disappeared into the air.

"You all wait here a sec," Robin said as she climbed up on top of the breakwater. "I've got an idea!"

With the flashlight playing on the stones ahead of her, she made her way back to where the structure ended in a stand of low-growing scrub pines about fifty feet from the edge of the sea. Here she stopped and trained the light on the ground around her.

"Yippee!" she yelled. "My hunch was right!"

Quickly jumping off the stones, she ran back across the beach.

"What was your hunch, Robin?" Michael called out as he ran toward the approaching light.

Mindy and the others followed close behind him, all shouting questions in their eagerness to find out what Robin had discovered.

"More tracks!" she cried breathlessly. "Our Phantom must have jumped up on the jetty like I did, then run along it so he wouldn't leave any tracks in the sand. Then he must have made his way through the woods to the road."

"That's a plausible explanation, I must say," her father remarked, "but it also means the end of this particular trail, my dear."

"I know," Robin said with a sigh, turning back toward the terrace. "Another dead end. Let's have a look at the telephone wire. Show me where it is, will you, Mike?"

Michael led the way around the corner of the house to the rose garden and pointed out the connection near the base of the house. The others stood in a little cluster on the brick path as Robin picked her way through the rosebushes and flashed a beam of light first on the broken wire and then on the ground around her. The gardener had mulched the rose beds with buckwheat hulls, which made it difficult for footprints to show, but after a careful search, Robin noticed one place, which hadn't been entirely covered by the mulch, where a part of the same webbed imprint was dimly visible.

"This proves that the phone was put out of commission by that thing Manuela saw," Robin cried. "You can call it a ghost or an ostrich or whatever you like, but *I* know it was the Phantom."

"You may be right, Robin," her father said. "I wonder if we shouldn't report this to the police?"

"Oh, no, Daddy," Robin protested emphatically. "You know the Phantom probably won't be around here again tonight. He wouldn't run the risk of being caught, so I think we should all try to relax and get to bed."

"I think Robin's right, sir," Michael said, "especially since Dad wants to avoid calling attention to what's been going on lately. I'm sure we aren't in the slightest danger."

"How about you, Manuela?" Mr. Kane asked. "Would you feel more comfortable if you all came back to our house for the night?"

"Oh, no! *Gracias, Señor* Kane!" Manuela said, straightening up to her full height and folding her arms resolutely in front of her. "I stay here! Robin is right, I know. There will be no more ghosts tonight. With Michael back, I feel safe again."

"I wish *I* felt that safe!" Mindy said. "I must confess that I feel jumpy as a cat. If the invitation is still open, *I'm* going to say 'yes' and spend the night at Robin's house."

"Oh, good!" Robin cried. "That will give us a chance to talk about—"

"You two have to promise not to talk about *any-thing* until dawn." Mr. Kane laughed. "It's almost midnight and tomorrow is a school day. Come on. It's home for us in a hurry."

While Mindy went to get her nightgown and toilet articles, Mr. Kane and the others accompanied Manuela through the house as she went from room to room turning off the lights and seeing that everything was in order. By the time they were all back in the hall, Robin was sure that Manuela was in full control of herself again.

"Good night, Manuela! Good night, Mike!" she called out as she headed for the car. "See you to-morrow!"

8.

A Cookout

O NCE BACK at the Kanes', Mindy and Robin lost no time getting settled for the night. It was not only that they had given Mr. Kane their word to go right to bed, but, in addition, as they both reluctantly admitted, they were really exhausted. In fact, Robin was so tired that she couldn't fall asleep immediately. She lay quietly until she knew from Mindy's steady breathing that she was asleep. Then she reached over to her bedside table for a drink of water, closed her eyes tightly, and started the old trick of counting sheep. Next morning she found she

106

couldn't remember how far she had gotten before sleep overtook her.

Mrs. Kane was filling Amy's bowl with hot oatmeal as the girls came into the kitchen.

"I was just about to call you," she said cheerily, "but I wanted to wait until the last minute before interrupting your beauty sleep. I must say, you both look as fresh as though you'd gone to bed at eight. That's youthful vigor for you!"

"Speaking of youthful vigor, where's Kev?" Robin asked. "In all the excitement last night I forgot to ask him about the tryouts. I wonder how he came out."

"He made the first team," Amy piped up, "and so did my friend Joe!"

"Yippee!" Robin shouted, grabbing Mindy and whirling her gaily around the kitchen.

"Watch it, girls!" Mrs. Kane warned as they almost upset the tray of glasses she was carrying. "Here comes our football hero now! He's already been out doing a little running to get in condition."

Kevin came into the kitchen slightly out of breath, his cheeks red. Skipping gracefully on tiptoe from one foot to the other, he made a few jabs at an imaginary punching bag, then sat down for breakfast.

"Congratulations, Kev. I *knew* you'd make the team!" Mindy said. "I'll come to every single game and cheer for you."

"Thanks, Mindy," Kevin replied with a warm smile.

"We'll need all the encouragement we can get this year. There are a lot of new fellows on the team because several of the regulars graduated last June."

"Do you think Joe will work out all right, not knowing much about the game and all?" Mindy asked.

"He'll be the best one on the whole team!" Amy managed to say despite a mouthful of cereal.

"You're right, Sugar; you don't have to worry about Joe," Kevin said. "He's a natural athlete and he's already boning up on the rules."

"Oh, speaking of Joe, I hope he and his uncle will be here for dinner tonight," Mrs. Kane said. "Mr. Turner hasn't had a phone put in yet, so I couldn't talk to him, but I asked Joe when he stopped by yesterday afternoon. He said he'd let me know if they couldn't make it, and since I didn't hear from him, I assume the party's on."

"And can I assume Mindy and Mike are coming, too?" Robin asked with a smile. "It wouldn't be a party without them."

"Of course, dear!" Mrs. Kane replied. "You two are free tonight, aren't you, Mindy?"

"You know we're always free when Daddy's away," Mindy said, a touch of sadness in her voice. "Mike and I would love to come. Is it a cookout, Mrs. Kane?"

"Would you like that, Mindy?" Mrs. Kane asked. "I thought you might be getting tired of our alfresco dining habits."

"Never!" Mindy exclaimed. "Everything seems to

taste better outdoors. What time do you want us to be here?"

"Oh, anytime around six thirty, or earlier if you like."

After breakfast Mindy started to clear the table, but Mrs. Kane thanked her for offering to help, then whisked everyone out of the kitchen, saying it was time they were on their way to school.

By the time they had reached the gates of the junior-senior high, Robin, with suggestions from Mindy and Kevin, had worked out the wording of the announcement about the competition.

"I have a free study period the first thing this morning," Mindy said, "so I can print up two or three posters if you want me to."

"Oh, that's wonderful!" Robin answered. "You're so good at art, Mindy. My printing always gets smudgy, or goes downhill, or runs off the edge of the paper."

"You'd better put one on each bulletin board and one in the art room," Kevin suggested, "and we can also talk it up to all our friends."

"I'm going to phone Daddy during lunch hour, and check with him," Mindy said. "Why don't you meet me in the cafeteria, Robin, so you can hear what he has to say?"

"And I'll hunt up Mike and bring him up to date on our plans," Kevin said. "Golly! I can't wait until Saturday to see what happens!"

The three parted to go to their respective home-rooms, each wondering if the day would ever end. The excitement of their project, plus the anticipation of the forthcoming scuba party, made it difficult for any of them to concentrate on lessons.

When the noon bell finally sounded, Robin hurried to the school lunchroom to find Mindy. She was already there, the finished posters tucked under her arm.

"Grab a tray and get in line so we won't waste any time," Robin urged her friend.

They decided to skip dessert, so, within a few minutes after finishing their tuna-fish sandwiches and salad, they were heading for the phone. They both squeezed into the booth and were barely able to close the door.

"I guess it's lucky we *didn't* eat that chocolate pudding," Robin remarked with a chuckle, "or we'd be stuck in here for good!"

When Mindy started to tell her father about the footprints they had seen the previous night, he interrupted her to say that Michael had already phoned him.

"I should have known Mike would think of calling you the first thing," Mindy said. "Now Robin and I want to read you what we're putting on the posters."

When she had finished, he said, "Sounds fine to me. You've covered the reason for the show, the time, the place, and the free admission. There's just one other thing. Don't you think there ought to be a prize?"

"Oh, that's a great idea!" Robin, her ear close to the phone, exclaimed. "We hadn't thought of that, but it certainly would get more people interested in entering the contest."

"I'll contribute fifty dollars to the winner," Mr. Hunter said. "Mr. and Mrs. Kane can act as judges, and we'll keep the names of the artists secret until after they announce the winner. That way it will be perfectly fair."

"I can easily add the information about the prize on the bottom of the posters, Daddy," Mindy told him. "Are you going to announce the competition down there, too?"

"I spoke about it to the makeup director this morning, and apparently the word has spread like wildfire," Mr. Hunter told her. "Six or seven people have already asked me for details."

"Tell him Daddy's going to try to get it into the *Chronicle,* too," Robin whispered to Mindy, "so everyone can read about it tonight. We want to make sure the Phantom knows all about it!"

"Fine, Mindy. The more publicity we get, the better," Mr. Hunter said. "I hope we'll have room to hang all the entries."

The warning bell for afternoon classes interrupted their conversation, so after promising to phone again later on, Mindy hung up.

"Meet you under the live oak tree after school," Robin called as they went their separate ways down the long hall.

Although Mrs. Kane spent many hours working on the lovely driftwood figurines she sold to a store in San Francisco, and tending to her rose garden, her household ran smoothly and she always seemed to find time to entertain her children's friends. Her warm hospitality was one reason why the Kane home was a favorite place for the young people to gather.

When Robin came into the patio after school, she found her mother in an old pair of dungarees, a smudge of dirt on the tip of her nose. She was clipping the faded blooms from the beautiful Belle of Portugal rambler which covered one side of Mr. Kane's studio.

"Mom, the patio looks absolutely marvelous!" Robin exclaimed as she looked around at the well-tended rose beds and the newly pruned vines. "You must have been working all day. Why, even the swimming pool has been de-leafed!"

"It does look better, doesn't it?" Mrs. Kane laughingly replied as she surveyed her work. "It was long overdue, I'm afraid. I figured that with the exhibition coming up, today was as good a time as any to have a cleanup drive."

"Has Dad seen it?" Robin asked. "He'll be simply flabbergasted!"

"Oh, he cleaned out the pool," her mother replied. "You know, that's really Kevin's job, but he's so involved with football these days that he's let his chores slip a bit."

"Jiminy crickets! That reminds me—this is my day to help out at the library. Do you need me before six?"

"No, dear. I got the hamburgers ready this morning and made the potato salad, so there's nothing more to do until later. You run along," Mrs. Kane said. "I know how much Mrs. Norville depends on you volunteers to keep the shelves in order."

When Robin finally returned home, she had just enough time to take a quick shower and get into fresh clothes before the arrival of Mindy and Michael. On an impulse she decided against wearing shorts and put on a new flowered sheath she had not yet worn. The soft coral, green, and beige colors of the print complemented her brown hair and tanned skin, and Robin, who usually was quite unconcerned about her appearance, took an appraising look in the mirror.

Not bad! she said to herself. *It actually makes me look slim!*

When she saw that Mindy was also wearing a dress, she was doubly glad she had decided against shorts. Dressing up made even a cookout seem festive.

"Hey, Robin, I *like* that!" Michael said as Robin came out to greet her friends.

It was not many minutes after six thirty when Joe

arrived with his uncle. Robin was immediately struck with the dissimilarity of their appearances. Whereas Joe was husky in build and had reddish hair and deep-set brown eyes, Mr. Turner was thin and fair-skinned. His chin was covered by a beard, its heavy growth contrasting oddly with his sparse blond hair. Heavy glasses seemed to emphasize the blueness of his small eyes. Robin guessed that he was in his early forties. He thanked Mrs. Kane profusely for her invitation after Joe had introduced them, and he greeted Mr. Kane with a friendly handshake.

"Joe has told me about you all, especially Amy," he remarked as he met the others. "It's been a break for Joe to have friends this close, because my work has kept me from spending as much time as I should like with him."

"We love to have Joe over here anytime," Mrs. Kane said as she poured tomato-juice cocktails for her guests. "He's told us about your writing. Architecture must be a fascinating subject to work on."

Mr. Turner agreed that his research had been most interesting. Then he quickly changed the subject by asking Mr. Kane about *his* work.

"I'm a regular reader of your strip, 'Family Scene,'" he remarked, "and it beats me how you can come up with a new idea every day. I'm afraid I wouldn't have enough imagination for that sort of thing."

"Well, my own family keeps me pretty well supplied

with ideas," Mr. Kane replied. "They're usually involved in something that makes a good story."

"As a matter of fact, we're busy right now on planning an art contest," Robin said. "Mindy's father is sponsoring it, in connection with a television series on the California missions which he's directing."

"Yes, I heard something about it," Mr. Turner replied. "The series, I mean. Tell me more about the contest. It sounds like quite an original idea."

"I saw the posters at school today," Joe said. "I'd like to try to dream up something to enter, but I can't draw a straight line!"

They told Mr. Turner more about the contest while they were waiting for the charcoal to burn down to the proper glow for cooking the hamburgers. Joe's uncle was enthusiastic about the project. He even offered to take time off from his writing to give them a hand setting up the show.

"We may *have* to call on you," Robin said. "It all depends on the number of entries we get. They're all supposed to be here by ten o'clock Saturday morning, and Open House is from four to five. So you see we don't have too much time to get them all hung."

The boys had gathered around the two *brazeros* which the Kanes often used instead of the grill to cook the meat. Joe had never seen one before, and he was fascinated by the efficient little red pottery cooking devices which Kevin told him were used extensively by the Mexicans to cook their food.

"You see, it's sort of a large clay hourglass," Michael explained, "and you get a good draft from this moon-shaped opening in the bottom part. They're really great because they don't weigh more than a few pounds. They're inexpensive and easy to use, and a little charcoal goes a long way."

"We sometimes take ours to the beach for picnics," Amy, who managed to stay close to Joe, remarked, "and when we're through cooking, we just dump out the coals and cover them with sand."

"I'd like to send one of those to my family," Joe said. "Who knows, it might start a new fad in staid old England."

While they were talking, Kevin was making ineffectual pokes at the charcoal in an effort to hurry the fire along.

"Kevin, won't you ever learn that poking won't do a bit of good?" Mr. Kane said good-humoredly, waving a palm leaf in front of the *brazero* to increase the draft.

"Well, I'm dying of hunger," Kevin moaned. "I could eat an old shoe at this point."

"Well, bear up for ten minutes," Mr. Kane chuckled. "I think the hamburgers can go on now."

Mrs. Kane brought over a tray on which she had stacked the patties.

"Those smell wonderful even before they're cooked," Joe remarked as she removed the waxed paper with which they were covered.

"They're Mom's special!" Robin said. "Chopped onion and catsup and I don't know what all she puts in to make them so good."

Robin and Mindy gathered up the juice glasses and carried them into the kitchen while the meat was cooking. Mrs. Kane had already gone in to get the salad and pickles out of the refrigerator, and the buttered rolls from the heating oven. By the time the girls had arranged the dishes and silver at the tables, the hamburgers were done.

Conversation ebbed somewhat as everyone settled down to enjoy the meal. Mr. Kane was kept busy grilling more hamburgers, and Robin saw to it that the salad bowl was passed around. Finally Amy, who had managed to eat two of the juicy patties and an extra-large helping of potato salad, piped up, "What's for dessert, Mom?"

"Don't tell me you have any room left, Amy!" Joe laughed. "I haven't eaten like this since—well, not since I had Mrs. Kane's chili two nights ago."

"I thought it might be fun for each one to make his own sundae tonight," Mrs. Kane said.

She brought out a large bowl of ice cream, half vanilla and half chocolate, and a tray on which there were a variety of sauces—butterscotch, marshmallow, fudge, and maple-walnut. Robin followed with the dessert dishes and spoons. Everyone, including Joe, found he could still enjoy this special treat, and there was much laughter at some of the concoctions.

When dinner was over, it was almost dark, and Mr. Kane lighted the pierced tin lanterns that hung around the patio. After the tables had been cleared and put away, everyone relaxed in the comfortable redwood chairs and chaises near the pool.

"Kev, didn't I see a guitar in your room the other day?" Joe asked. "Do you play it?"

"Oh, I make a stab at it," Kevin answered modestly.

"What do you mean, Kevin Kane!" Mindy cried. "He's the best player in the whole school, and maybe in the whole world! Bring it out, Kev, and play for us."

Kevin, embarrassed by Mindy's glowing praise, was glad for a chance to escape into the house. When he came back a few minutes later, he strummed the instrument to get it in tune, then, standing with one foot on the edge of a chair, he began to play some desultory chords followed by an intricate Spanish composition. His playing brought cheers from everyone.

"I'm not going to do all the work," Kevin said with a smile after he had thanked them for their ovation. "How about all of you joining in this next one?"

He began singing the familiar "Sweet Betsy From Pike," and by the time he had got to the chorus everyone except Joe was singing. It didn't take Joe long to pick up the tune, however, and soon he was singing as lustily as anyone.

Time sped by all too fast, as it always did when Kevin played, and it was not until Mr. Turner, looking at his wristwatch, said it was time to be going that anyone realized how late it was.

"Luckily tomorrow is a school holiday," Robin said, "but we still have to get up early to get down to Breakwater. We'll pick you up a little before eight, Joe. Okay?"

"Right, Robin! I'm looking forward to my first dip in the Pacific."

Joe and his uncle thanked the Kanes over and over again for the wonderful evening.

"In a week or so I hope to get things in shape at our house. Then we can be a bit more hospitable," Mr. Turner said. "I have found there's a lot more to do than I anticipated."

"I should imagine so," Mrs. Kane replied, "with the place being unoccupied for so long. Do let us know if we can be of any help. We want to be good neighbors."

After Joe and Mr. Turner left, Mindy and Michael made their own farewells, Mindy giving Mrs. Kane a warm kiss.

"I guess I'll call you my almost-mother," she said, "and Robin will be my almost-sister."

"Does that make me an almost-anything?" Michael asked quickly. He had sensed the sadness in his sister's question and was trying to end the party on a cheerful note.

"You can be almost anything you want, Mike,"
Robin quipped as her two best friends headed for
home. "Now don't oversleep, you two. Tomorrow's
a big day!"

9.

Skin Diving

THURSDAY MORNING was bright and warm, and Robin was awake before seven despite the fact that excitement had kept her from sleeping as soundly as usual. She took a quick shower and put on her swimsuit, a pair of faded blue denim shorts, and one of her father's old shirts, tying the tails tightly around her waist and rolling the sleeves above her elbows.

"Thank goodness I don't have to bother with braids or curlers," she thought to herself as she sat down at her dressing table and ran a comb through her short curls. "But I *do* wish I didn't have such a polka-dot nose!"

She briefly surveyed the golden dust of freckles which everyone else found quite attractive but which was an occasional source of annoyance to Robin. She didn't let it bother her for long, however, and after making her bed and giving her room a semblance of order, she ran down the hall to her brother's room. Getting no response from a knock on the door, she opened it and looked in.

"How can anyone sleep that soundly," she muttered, going over to the bed and giving his shoulders a shake, "especially with such a big day ahead."

Kevin mumbled something unintelligible and pulled the blanket over his head. Tramp, who had heard Robin's footsteps, came in at that moment, his tail wagging with joy.

"Go get him, Tramp!" Robin ordered, pointing to her comatose brother.

In one bound Tramp landed on the bed and began to pull at the covers.

"Okay, okay!" Kevin cried, sitting up and wrestling playfully with their beloved pet. "You win! I'll get right up. Now out of here, both of you. Can't you let a fella dress in peace?"

Robin was so excited over the prospect of skin diving that she resented having to take time for breakfast, but she knew that her brother was hungry as a bear in the morning. Besides, she had promised her mother the night before to eat something before she left for Breakwater. She headed for the kitchen, followed by Tramp, who, as usual, was looking for a handout. By the time she had poured the orange juice, filled two bowls with cereal and sliced bananas, and brought a large pitcher of milk from the refrigerator, Kevin appeared.

After breakfast, as they were rinsing the dishes and loading them into the dishwasher, Robin caught the deep roar of the bullhorn from the Heap.

"There's Mindy and Mike now," she said, hurriedly wiping her hands.

"That horn's enough to wake the dead!" Kevin laughed as he tossed a sweater over his shoulder and headed outside.

Robin followed, giving Tramp a gentle push away from the door. He responded with a howl of disappointment, his canine sixth sense telling him he was about to miss something special.

"Let's take him along," Robin said. "He loves the water, and Michael and Mindy won't mind. He's almost as much their dog as ours."

"Okay, fella!" Kevin called out to him. Robin held the door open and Tramp shot through it and headed for the station wagon, where he received a loud welcome from Mindy and her brother.

When they got to Joe's house they found him waiting for them outside the gate, his frogman equipment on the curb beside him.

"You needn't have lugged all that out here," Michael said, getting out of the car to help load up. "I would have driven up to the house."

"I know you would, old man," Joe replied with a trace of embarrassment, "but I didn't want to take a chance on disturbing Uncle George. He made it rather plain last night that he didn't want to be bothered."

"What do you mean?" Robin asked. "He wasn't *mad* at you, was he?"

Joe kicked a pebble down the sidewalk and thrust his hands almost angrily into his pockets.

"If he wasn't, I don't know what you'd call it. I went up to his room before going to bed last night to tell him about our plans for today. When he heard me he opened the door just a crack and told me he never wanted to see me in the tower again. I guess writers are under quite a strain, so I try not to let it bother me."

"I should say his reaction was pretty extreme, writer or no writer," Robin said positively. "It's a good thing he doesn't live in *our* house. I guess we're the noisiest family in all Pacific Point!"

While they were talking, Michael and Kevin had stowed away things in the station wagon. When they got back in the car Robin moved over to make room for Joe beside her in the front seat.

"Well, you're a family," Joe said, a bit despondently, "like mine in England. My sister and brother are always whooping it up, but my uncle—" Shaking his head in obvious perplexity, Joe left the sentence unfinished.

"But he seemed so pleasant last night," Robin said, "the way he offered to help us with the exhibit and all."

"Did he *really* say he'd help you?" Joe asked incredulously. "I didn't hear him. Well, maybe he'll warm up in time. I'll try to be patient."

"In the meantime, you can be part of *our* family, like Mike and Mindy," Robin said warmly. "The more the merrier!"

"That's good of you," Joe replied. "I'm afraid I'd have had a real case of homesickness without all of you to cheer me up. I don't know how I'll ever repay your kindness."

"Repay us!" Robin cried. "Why, scuba lessons alone are more than enough—as though we needed any repayment."

"Hey, Mike, can't you drive any faster, for pete's sake?" Kevin broke in. "I don't want to waste the whole day getting down to Breakwater."

"I *could* drive faster for *pete's* sake," Michael laughed, "but for our own sakes I'm going to keep within the speed limit. After all, it isn't nine o'clock yet."

The little town of Breakwater was just waking up. As they drove along the main street they saw Nick in his big white apron putting up a menu of the day's specials in the window of his restaurant. The town's only grocer was arranging a tempting array of fresh vegetables and fruits outside his store, and Sheriff Jackson was running up the flag in front of his office. He waved as he recognized Robin and Mindy in the Heap.

"Jiminy, I wonder if we'll have to ask him for help again," Robin mused. "If many more things happen to delay the shooting of the picture I should think that Mr. Hunter would *have* to report it to Sheriff Jackson."

"Well, Sheriff Jackson actually wasn't much help with El Gato," Michael reminded her. "It was *you* who got on his trail, remember?"

"Yes, Robin," Mindy said, "and I have a feeling Daddy thinks you'll get to the root of all this funny business, too."

"Let's keep our eyes peeled today," Robin urged them. "Everyone will think we're down here just for the fun of it, so maybe we can get some leads. It's about time we found out something!"

As they approached the old pier and nearby mission, everything was humming. Mindy and Michael said they scarcely recognized the place that had seemed so quiet when they had visited it with their father. Robin and Kevin were surprised at the reconstructed chapel, a bell hanging in the once empty arch high above the door, and the freshly stuccoed white walls.

The big cameras were being wheeled into position on their dollies. Crowds of extras, dressed as monks and fishermen, were milling around. Joe, who had never been on a movie set before, was fascinated by it all.

"See those men over there, the ones shifting that piece of scenery that looks like a stone wall?" Robin asked. "They're called 'grips.' The ones who work with the lights and electrical equipment are 'juicers.' There's a whole strange vocabulary in the movie world."

Mindy spotted her father, script in hand, in the midst of a group of actors. When he caught sight of them, he dropped the script into a chair and hurried over to them.

"Is everything going all right, Mr. Hunter?" Robin asked after greetings had been exchanged. "Have you had any more delays?"

"No, my dear. Everything went well yesterday; we got a lot done. Today we're filming external shots around the chapel. But time is running out, and if San Andrea's fish doesn't show up soon we'll be in trouble."

"Couldn't you just use a fake instead?" Michael suggested.

"Oh, I suppose we *could* as a last resort," his father said, "but this whole episode centers on the fish. It, above all things, should be completely authentic. Besides, it would take time to have a satisfactory facsimile of anything as intricate as that made."

As they were talking, Robin's eyes were taking in every detail of the scene around her. She realized that any one of the many people involved in the making of the picture could be the guilty one. Noticing her preoccupation, Mr. Hunter asked, "Any ideas, Robin?"

"Not yet, I'm afraid," she said, shaking her head. "But ever since we found the box in the Heap I've had an awfully strong hunch that the fish is somewhere around the set."

"What makes you think that?" Mindy asked. "It could be in Timbuktu for all we know." She shrugged despairingly.

"Perhaps," Robin conceded, "but taking into consideration everything else that's happened, I can't believe the Phantom took the fish for any reason other than to delay your film, Mr. Hunter." She paused.

"So?" Kevin urged her on.

"So, he'd be apt to get rid of it right away, even though he planned to use the box it was in as a red herring back in Pacific Point." She paused and with a smile said, "Of course, as I said before, it's just a hunch."

"Hunches sometimes pay off, Robin, old girl," Michael said. "Remember the bird tracks!"

"Well, try to have fun today, anyway," Mr. Hunter

urged them. "The other skin-diving suit and the rest of the gear is in my office over by the landing. I'll send one of the boys to unlock the door for you. Now be careful, all of you. Be sure you don't take any chances."

"Don't worry, sir," Joe assured him. "The first rule for any frogman is just that—don't take any chances."

"If you'll excuse me, I'd better be getting back to the set," Mr. Hunter said. "Every minute counts, you know. See you all later."

"Come on. Let's go down to the water before we pick up our gear," Robin suggested. "Joe can decide the best place for us to go in. I'm so anxious for us to get started."

By now the sun was quite high in the sky, and only a faint breeze rippled the surface of the water. Miniature waves broke at the edge of the beach, leaving scallops of foam as they receded. Robin kicked off her loafers and began to wiggle her toes in the warm sand.

"How about going in here?" Michael asked. "Or is it too shallow?"

"We'd have to wade out a good distance to reach a decent depth," Joe replied, looking around. "How about that old pier over there? We could go off the end of it if there's any way that we could get down to the water."

"Let's go see!" Kevin cried enthusiastically, starting

on a run down the beach. The others followed his lead.

"It couldn't be better," Joe declared after surveying the dock. He shied a pebble out into the water and watched it sink. "It's plenty deep out here. I've never seen water this clear! Those shells and stones on the bottom show up plain as day."

"And here are some steps, such as they are," Robin called out.

She had knelt down on the edge of the catwalk and was examining some rough boards nailed between two of the pilings so that they formed a crude ladder to the water.

"They seem sturdy enough," Joe announced after taking a step down to see if they would bear his weight. "Good luck! Let's go get the suits."

They parked the Heap near Mr. Hunter's improvised office and started to unpack. It wasn't long before a tall, good-looking young man, dressed in gray flannels and a bright sport shirt, came running up to the shed. He greeted them pleasantly and, after making some casual remarks about the weather, started up the rickety steps.

Robin, as inconspicuously as possible, left the others and sauntered over to the shed, her hands clasped behind her back.

"My goodness, what a lot of keys!" she said, trying not to look too curious. "How do you ever remember which one unlocks what?"

"I don't have to know 'em all," the young man answered with a smile. "These here are Mr. Hunter's keys, and I just have to remember this new brass one is for the office padlock."

He turned his attention to the door, opened it, and pocketed the key ring.

"I'll be back later and lock up," he said. "I've got some errands to run and I might as well do it while you kids are getting your stuff out."

Hm, he said he doesn't have to know what all the keys are for, Robin thought to herself, *but what's to keep him from finding out if he wanted to? I wonder if anyone else has such easy access to Mr. Hunter's keys.*

As she pondered these questions, head bent and hands clasped behind her back, Robin wandered toward the old pier. She was brought up short when she suddenly stubbed her toe against a half-buried piece of driftwood.

"Ouch!" she cried, jumping up and down on one foot. Remembering she had left her loafers down on the beach, she ran off, limping slightly, to retrieve them.

She was heading back to the shack when her attention was suddenly caught by one of the monks. He had left a group of similarly clad extras who were lounging around the beach waiting to go on the set. Now he was walking hurriedly out on the pier.

I wonder what he's up to, Robin thought as she

slowed to a walk. Her curiosity was further aroused when he stopped suddenly, looked quickly around, and then, kneeling down, leaned over the edge of the catwalk. He seemed to study the water intently near one of the pilings. Then he got up and ran back to mingle with the other extras.

That's odd! I'll have to see what's out there, Robin said to herself, making a mental note of just where the man had stopped.

Her speculations were interrupted by Kevin's calling out to her from the door of the shed. "Come on, slacker!" he said. "Give Mindy a hand with this aqualung. We haven't got all day, for pete's sake!"

"Oh, you and your imaginary pal Pete!" Robin laughed as she ran up the steps. "Trust you brawny males to cope with the fins and leave the heavy equipment to us girls."

"Joe says the whole rig weighs only about thirty pounds, dear sister," Kevin called back over his shoulder as he passed her on the stairs and headed for the landing. "We're saving *our* strength for diving!"

"What!" Robin's cry sounded so indignant that it brought her brother up short in his tracks. "If you think for one minute, Kevin Kane, that Mindy and I aren't going to get into diving suits, too, you're crazy!"

"Oh, Robin, you always take Kevin too seriously," Mindy chuckled. "He was only teasing you."

"What a sense of humor!" Robin grumbled. "Will I ever learn not to fall for his kidding?"

The bantering stopped as they gathered around Joe. He was already pulling off his shirt and dungarees, preparing to put on his frogman suit.

As Robin watched him, an uneasy thought crossed her mind. Try as she would to suppress it, it kept haunting her. Where had Joe been the night Manuela and the servants had been so frightened? Joe and Kevin had had football tryouts that afternoon—the same afternoon she and Mindy and Mike had driven to the ranch—but then where had he gone? Only someone experienced in using fins could have run with the speed Manuela had described.

It couldn't be Joe! she said to herself. *There are loads of other people around Pacific Point who use fins.* But once having thought of it, the suspicion was difficult to suppress. Just then Kevin interrupted her train of thought.

"Who goes first?" he asked, scarcely able to suppress his excitement.

"Let's draw lots. That's the only fair way," Mindy said.

"Why not leave it to Joe to decide?" Robin suggested. "After all, he's our leader." She drew herself up sharply and gave a brisk salute.

"Hold everything, me hearties," Joe answered with a smile. "Before anyone has a try at skin diving he has to pass a swimming test."

"But you *know* we can all swim," Kevin said, a note of impatience in his voice.

"Sure, sure, old man." Joe gave him a gentle slap on the shoulder. "But I have to see that you can swim fifty yards underwater, and not just the length of a swimming pool. Now into the briny, and swim out to that rock. It looks to be about fifty yards away, and no bobbing up for air. Understand?"

He pointed to a large, flat-topped rock, which was well offshore.

"Oh, that's a cinch," Kevin said, stripping down to his swimming trunks. "I can do that in two seconds flat!"

Tramp had already gone for a swim. He was poised to jump in again, but when Robin ordered him to stay behind, he shook himself vigorously, spattering water on all of them, and trotted off to dig for imaginary gophers in the sand.

Michael took a deep breath and dived in first, swimming slowly about half a yard below the surface. He was pacing himself, for he knew the rock wasn't as close as it looked from the shore. He hadn't gone very far before he noticed Kevin churning rapidly past him.

He'd better take it easy, Michael thought to himself. *He's got a long haul ahead.*

When he looked back to check on the two girls he saw that they were making good progress, both swimming easily just under the surface. As he swam steadily on, his need for air became more and more intense. He felt as though his lungs would explode if he didn't surface and take a breath. He let a little air out of his lungs to lighten the pressure, and with one last burst of energy shot through the water toward the gray mass in front of him—the rock. He pulled himself slowly up on the warm stone, trying not to pant too hard as the cool air flooded into his lungs.

Kevin, he saw, was already there. He was lying flat on his back, his arms flung over his head, his eyes closed.

"Are you all right?" Michael asked, anxiously kneeling beside the prostrate figure.

"I will be in a sec," Kevin managed to answer between gasps. "Are the girls—"

"They're right here, Kev. You just stay quiet. Everything is all right." The last remark was as much to reassure Robin and Mindy as Kevin, for the two girls, breathless as they climbed out of the water, showed immediate concern over Kevin. "He's a bit winded, but he'll be okay in a little while," Michael told them in a low voice.

They waited for some time before deciding they were rested enough to swim back to the landing. Then, at the last minute, Kevin said he thought he would wait a little while longer before making the return trip. Michael was reluctant to let Kevin swim back alone, but he knew he was a superb swimmer even though he didn't always use the best judgment.

It won't hurt him to find out that his strength and his wind have limits, Michael thought to himself.

He beckoned Robin and Mindy to start back with him. Trusting his judgment, they followed his lead and headed for the landing.

Joe was waiting for them, a worried look on his face. He gave a hand to the girls as they climbed up the ladder.

"I see Kevin ran into trouble," Joe said. "I was afraid that his enthusiasm might possibly play tricks on him."

"You mean he had to come up before he got to the rock?" Robin asked.

"Anyone would have had to, going at that speed," Joe told her.

"Is that why you made us all take the test?" Mindy queried.

"Not entirely. I would have had you go through it anyway," Joe replied soberly, "but I also wanted to teach Kevin a very important lesson. I felt this was the only way to do it. I hate to admit it, but I had to learn the same thing in the same way in Oslo last summer. I thought I knew a lot more about my swimming ability than my instructor."

"But will Kev be able to try a dive today?" Robin asked, concerned that her brother might miss out on the fun.

"I'm afraid not, Robin," Joe replied. "Skin diving

is not child's play. It's a lot of fun, yes, but it can be dangerous, too. Kevin's got to realize that. If he has to wait until next time, he'll think twice the rest of his life before taking a risk. Do you think I'm right, Mike?"

"I'll go along with that," Michael said, "but I'd hate to be the one who has to tell him he's got to wait until next time!"

Michael, hands on his hips, looked out toward the rock. The others followed his glance and saw Kevin already starting back, taking his time now, but swimming steadily with a powerful crawl.

"You know, that boy swims like a seal," Joe remarked as he watched Kevin. "I'll wager he'll make a cracking good diver."

As it turned out, no one had to tell Kevin that he had lost his chance for a turn with the diving suit. He was a good enough athlete to know he had made a serious error in judgment. As he pulled himself up the ladder he looked a little shamefaced. Once on the landing, he held up his hand and shook his head. "Don't say it!" he said ruefully. "I've learned my lesson the hard way. Me for the doghouse this trip, eh, Joe?"

Joe nodded his head slowly. Relief swept over the little group, and Robin, feeling close to tears but full of pride at her brother's show of character, gave a tremendous whoop. "Hurrah for Kevin! Three cheers for Kev!" Everyone joined in the shouting until Kevin yelled, "Hey, cut it out, all of you!"

He picked up the other suit and fins.

"Let's get someone into this monkey jacket," he grinned. "Let's not waste any more time, for pete's sake!"

10.

In the Water

IT WAS AGREED that Michael should take the first diving lesson. There was a good deal of laughter as he struggled to pull the tight neck of the suit over his head. When his face, red from the effort, finally emerged, Joe helped him fasten the closely fitting arm and neck bands. As he did this he explained that it was necessary to come up to the surface after the first dive in order to get as much air as possible out of the suit.

"Air inside hampers your descent," he said, "because it increases your buoyancy."

Next Joe demonstrated how the mouthpiece fitted back of the front teeth, and how it, as well as the face mask, could be removed under the surface and blown clear if water should get in.

"Here, I'll show you," he said, sticking his arms through the straps that held the heavy tank on his back. When it was in place, he pulled the air tubes over his head, bringing the mouthpiece into position. Then he put on the face mask, climbed down the ladder to the water level, and slipped into the sea. A trail of bubbles from the aqualung rose to the surface in the spot where he had gone down. It wasn't long before he came up to vent the air from his suit. Then, going under again, he showed them how to remove the mask and mouthpiece.

"Why didn't you put on this lead belt?" Robin asked when he had returned to the landing. "And how do you know how much lead to put in the little pockets?"

She held up one of the narrow canvas belts as she spoke.

"Ordinarily, you put in enough lead to maintain the right buoyancy at the level to which you plan to descend," Joe explained. "The deeper you go, the greater the pressure and the more lead you need."

"They measure the pressure in atmospheres, don't they?" Michael asked. "I read that somewhere."

"Right. When you're floating on the surface of the water you have one 'atmosphere' pressing on you.

Go down thirty feet and you add another, and so on. So you have to adjust the weight of the lead accordingly."

"Golly!" Kevin exclaimed. "It's complicated, isn't it?"

"There's a lot more to this business than meets the eye," Joe laughed. "You don't become a frogman just by buying the equipment. Today, however, we won't worry about the belts or the pressure gauges because we're not going to go very deep. The belts and gauges come later."

After he had instructed Michael in taking off his mask and mouthpiece, Joe checked his aqualung, climbed cautiously down the ladder, and lowered himself into the water. As Michael prepared to follow, Robin grabbed him impulsively by the arm.

"Mike, if you have a chance, take a look around that piling—the fifth one from the end. See if you notice anything unusual. I'll explain later."

"What's up?" Kevin asked, walking toward the spot his sister had indicated. "Another one of your hunches?"

"It's probably nothing," Robin replied. "Just an idea I had."

Their attention was diverted at this point by the two boys in the water. It was a little frightening to see how long they could stay under the surface. Although it was only a few minutes, it seemed to those watching to be much longer. Actually, Joe had told them, there was enough air in a full tank to last about twenty minutes.

On land the heavy equipment and fins had made the boys seem awkward, but once in the water they moved with the ease and grace of a fish. A slight kick with the frog feet was enough to impel them wherever they wanted to go. A trail of bubbles on the surface showed their course.

Over the years the accumulation of sand washing in from the sea had decreased the depth of the water around the old pier so that Michael and Joe were able to go to the floor of the ocean—about twenty feet down. Michael saw Joe motion to him to pick up a shell as he himself had done. He guessed that this might be the way to prove they had actually reached the bottom.

Michael was soon completely at ease in the water. He waved to Robin and began swimming in the direction of the piling she had pointed out. He and Joe disappeared under the dock for what, to Robin, seemed like ages. Then they swam slowly out into the open water; they kept close to the ocean floor, heads together, apparently combing the bottom. Suddenly Michael shot to the surface, seeming to erupt from the sea in one great burst of speed. With powerful strokes, he swam to the end of the dock.

He climbed up the ladder, tearing the mask from his face when he reached the top.

"Robin! Robin!" he cried breathlessly. "You'll

never believe it! You'll have to see for yourself!"

"What *is* it?" Robin exclaimed. "Tell me, for goodness' sake!"

"Robin, you've got to see this for yourself! Go on in! Joe will show you."

Michael had scarcely finished before Robin had peeled off her shirt and shorts and dived into the water. Joe was waiting for her, treading water. He immediately dived below, and Robin, taking a deep breath, went after him.

It took Joe only a second to locate the discovery. There, almost buried in the sand, Robin saw something bright. She grabbed at the glinting object, but the sand swirling around it threatened to obscure it. Robin surfaced to get another breath of air, and by the time she reached the bottom again the water had cleared. Joe was close by, but, knowing what lay on the bottom, he was letting Robin make the discovery for herself.

It was a beautiful, golden fish! *It must be San Andrea's fish,* Robin exulted. *It couldn't be any other.* A stout cord had been fastened through the ring in the fish's nose and tied to one of the pilings. Robin motioned for Joe to take hold of the cord while she once more shot to the surface for air. Her excitement seemed to cause her to use up the supply of oxygen in her lungs more quickly than usual.

When she reached the bottom again, Robin gently pulled the fish out of the sand. Joe tried to break the cord, but it was too strong. Robin swam with the fish under one arm, while Joe pulled up the cord, foot by foot, back to the piling.

"I think we found San Andrea's fish," Robin cried when she reached the dock. "It was out there in the water!"

Michael was already halfway down the ladder ready to give her a helping hand. The others were crowding around in great excitement, throwing out question after question.

"Whew! Let me get my breath," Robin gasped, wiping the water from her eyes.

"I guess Robin's hunch paid off," Michael said as Joe rejoined the group after untying the cord around the piling.

"It's either my hunch or the strangest coincidence in the world," Robin said, kneeling beside the fish and running her hands over the smooth gold scales.

"Isn't it the most beautiful thing you've ever seen?" Mindy asked softly. "And it's as bright and shining as ever! I've never been so happy in my whole entire life!"

"But what in the world made you ask me to look under that piling?" Michael asked. "You can't tell me you're that much of a clairvoyant!"

Robin gave a quick glance toward the shore before she answered. Then she told them about seeing the monk when she had gone to get her shoes.

"He just seemed to behave strangely," she said

simply. "I can't explain it any better than that. It was as if—looking back on it—as if he was checking to see if we had discovered the string leading to the fish."

"What did he look like?" Kevin asked excitedly.

"Honest, I don't know," Robin replied, exasperation sounding in her voice as she recalled how all the monks wore hoods that hid their faces. "I couldn't see his face from where I was standing, and by the time I'd returned to the shack he was lost among all the other extras."

"Do you think we ought to tell Mr. Hunter?" Joe asked. "Maybe we could catch him."

Robin didn't answer immediately. She was sitting with her arms clasped around her knees.

"What do you say, Sis?" Kevin prodded her.

"Give her time to think," Michael said. "I can almost hear the wheels going around in her head right now."

"They're going around awfully slowly!" Robin laughed. "But here's how I figure it. We certainly want to tell Mr. Hunter about finding the fish right away, but let's hold off about the monk."

"Why?" Mindy asked. "Here he is right under our noses and you want to hold off! I don't understand at all."

"Well, for one thing, I'm not sure he was doing anything more than looking at those little shiners swimming around the pier," Robin said. "And for another thing, if we get everyone all steamed up about the fish's being stolen, it will only cause another delay. The important thing is that the fish has been recovered."

"I think you're absolutely right, Robin," Michael agreed, "but I think we ought to get this to Dad right away, before anyone gets wind of our find. Fortunately, the whole crew is shooting over by the chapel right now."

"Let's not waste any more time, then. Let's take it to the shack. Come on!" Robin cried.

At this moment she suddenly looked at Mindy— Mindy, who had been so anxious to go skin diving, and who was now eagerly wrapping the fish in her own shirt.

"Wait a minute," Robin said. "A few minutes more won't make any difference. Mindy ought to have a chance to try the aqualung. After all, it was her father who got it for us."

"I wouldn't *dream* of such a thing!" Mindy protested. "We're taking the fish back right now, Robin Kane. Besides, it'll be more fun to keep Kevin company when he makes *his* first dive."

Robin didn't argue further with her friend. The sincerity of Mindy's words was obvious, and Robin knew it wasn't just excitement over finding the fish that made her forgo the diving lesson. More important, it was Mindy's growing awareness of other people. She was learning not to put herself first.

"Okay, if you say so," Robin said. "Mike, go find your father and bring him back to the shack. We'll meet you there."

Despite the warmth of the day and the excitement of finding the fish, Robin's teeth were chattering and, when she stood up, her legs felt so shaky that she didn't think she could take a step. Mindy noticed this and put a comforting arm around her friend's shoulder. In a few moments, however, Robin was herself again.

As they passed the Heap they saw that Tramp had jumped up on the open tail gate and was fast asleep. "I guess he gave up on us and wanted to be sure he wouldn't be left behind." Kevin gave the dog a gentle pat on the rump. Tramp responded with one thump of his tail, but slept on.

While they were waiting for Mr. Hunter and Michael to reach the shack, Robin unwrapped the fish. Mindy moved a small table into the middle of the room in front of the door.

"Let's put the fish here," she suggested. "Then Daddy will see it the minute he comes in." Mindy's eyes were sparkling.

They had barely completed the arrangement when they heard Mr. Hunter run up the steps. He took one look at the fish, then grabbed Robin and Mindy, each in one arm, and hugged them closely to him.

"I can't believe it!" he exclaimed. "I just can't believe it! Where in the world did you find it?"

"It's true, Daddy," Mindy said ecstatically. "Robin found it in the water near the old pier."

Mr. Hunter took the beautiful fish in his hands, turning it this way and that to assure himself it wasn't damaged.

"It's a good thing it's made of gold," Kevin said, "or the salt water might have corroded it."

"And it's a good thing, too, that your friend initiated you all into skin diving," Mr. Hunter said, smiling warmly at Joe. "Otherwise we might never have found our treasure."

"What are you going to do with it now, Mr. Hunter? You're not going to leave it here, are you?" Robin asked anxiously, remembering that the office had been left unlocked that morning while the young man with the keys was running errands.

"I'm not going to let it out of my sight!" Mr. Hunter assured her. "It's about lunchtime. Let's go down to Nick's and have a bite to eat. Then you can fill me in on all the details of your diving lesson *and* finding the fish."

"Daddy, I can't go out to lunch in my swimsuit and shorts!" Mindy said with a laugh. "I donated my shirt to cover up the fish."

"I've got an extra sweater in the car," Kevin volunteered. "I'll run and get it for you."

"And Joe and Mike have to get out of their scuba suits," Robin said. "I'm sure Nick wouldn't welcome them in that getup."

"Well, you all work out your various sartorial problems," Mr. Hunter chuckled, "and I'll be back in half an hour and pick you up."

He took the fish and returned it to its wooden box, which was on his desk, and, after wrapping the box in a piece of newspaper, tucked it carefully under his arm. He smiled warmly at the happy group around him.

The restaurant was not very crowded. The people working on the set ate at a special canteen, so only a handful of local people were eating at Nick's. When Nick saw them come in, he hurried out from behind the counter, pushed two tables together to make room for them, and flicked an imaginary crumb from the red and white tablecloth.

"What you like today, Mr. Hunter?" he asked, pointing to the menu displayed over the counter. "The eggplant and lamb—very good! But you have what you want."

Nick had been in Breakwater for many years, but he had never lost his Greek accent. Nor had he forgotten how to cook many delicious dishes from his native land. Hamburgers and chili were always on hand for those who wanted standard fare, but he was delighted when anyone ordered his Old World specialties.

"That sounds good to me," Mr. Hunter said. "How about you others?"

Kevin and Joe decided to stick with the usual hamburgers, but Michael and the girls, following Robin's lead, ordered the eggplant.

"I might as well be experimental," Robin said. "Otherwise I'll never be a cos— What's the word, Mr. Hunter?"

"I think you mean cosmopolite, Robin—that is to say, a citizen of the world."

"That's it!" she replied. "Then when I have to track down an international spy through a lot of foreign countries, I won't starve to death."

"Don't worry, Sis," Kevin said, shaking his head, "you'll never starve to death. At least not if I know you!"

As they were finishing their lunch Robin asked Mr. Hunter where he planned to keep the fish until it was needed for the filming.

"We don't want to run the risk of losing it again," she said, "and the shack doesn't seem a very safe place, does it?"

"No, my dear, experience has shown us that, all right," Mr. Hunter replied. "We might let the property man take charge of it; he has a trailer on the set."

"Do you have a key to that, too?" Robin asked. "As you do to your office?"

"No, the prop man is the only person who has one," he answered. "Why do you ask, Robin?"

Robin felt her cheeks flush. She didn't want to

seem impolite by criticizing Mindy's father, but she *did* think he was pretty careless with his keys. As tactfully as possible she pointed out that anyone could gain access to his office while it was left unlocked, even for a few minutes, as it had been that morning.

"You're right," Mr. Hunter said without any sign of resentment at the mild criticism. "I've always been careless about things like that, but I'll try to watch it in the future."

"How about letting Sheriff Jackson keep the fish?" Robin suggested. "I'm sure he has a safe in his office."

"Or he could put our finny friend behind bars in the local hoosegow," Kevin quipped. "I'll bet it would be the first time a thief has ever been locked *out* of jail."

Everyone laughed at Kevin's idea, but agreed that the sheriff's office *would* be a good place to leave the fish. They found Sheriff Jackson only too glad to take the responsibility when they called on him after lunch.

"There's not much doing around here anymore," he told them, "and time hangs heavy on my hands. Even guarding this for you will give me something to worry about. You know if a sheriff ain't worryin' about something, he's wasting the taxpayers' money."

After chatting a while Mr. Hunter handed over the fish and thanked him for his services, adding that he would like to stay longer but that he had to get back to the set. Everyone was in a gay mood as they drove back to the mission set, and, after saying good-bye to Mr. Hunter and gathering up their gear, they started for home.

11.

Getting Ready

"WHEN SHOULD we rig up the buzzer system in Daddy's studio?" Robin asked Mindy on the way to the Kanes' house after school the next day. "How can we do it without Joe's finding out about our plan? I've thought about letting him in on the scheme, but I just don't think it's a good idea. Why take a single chance we don't have to? We'd better keep the secret just between our two families."

"I was scared Daddy was going to spill the beans the other day at lunch when you were telling him about the monk you saw on the pier," Mindy said.

156

"Me, too! I was sure he was going to say something about our trap, but I managed to change the subject by asking where he planned to put the fish for safe-keeping."

The two friends walked on in silence for several minutes, each mentally going over the details of their plan.

"Mindy, I've been thinking." Robin suddenly broke the silence.

"You *have!*" Mindy laughed. "Who'd ever have guessed it?"

"No, seriously, Min, I've been so concerned about how our little plot would work that I've sort of over-looked the dangers. Even with Daddy there, things could happen awfully fast."

"*Very* fast," Mindy corrected her. "You're right, Robin; you *are* taking a big risk."

"I think we should tell Jerry Smith about our plan and ask him to stand by."

Jerry Smith was one of Pacific Point's three police officers, and he was a great favorite with the young people. He had grown up in the town and knew every-body. Robin and Mindy couldn't remember anyone else ever being on traffic duty outside the junior-senior high school.

"At last, Robin Kane, you're coming to your senses!" Mindy said with a sigh of relief. "That day you dashed off into the hills after El Gato I found out it was useless to argue with you—you just didn't seem to know the meaning of the word caution."

"Well, you see I'm learning," Robin chuckled.

When they reached home they found Kevin sitting at the kitchen table eating an enormous sandwich which he had made from an assortment of leftovers.

"That's what I call a king-size, super, deluxe hero!" Robin said. "Is there anything left for us?"

She poked her head into the refrigerator, and, finding nothing that appealed to her, she asked Mindy if she would settle for cookies and milk.

"Any time!" Mindy cried. "Your mother's cookies are better than any old sandwich."

"Where's Mom?" Robin asked her brother.

"Oh, Amy has another one of her overnight dates with Judy. Mom's driving her over. She'll be back pronto," Kevin said.

As Robin was pouring the milk, she told her brother about her decision to enlist Jerry's help. Kevin, like Mindy, gave immediate approval.

"I never did like the idea of the three of you having to cope with the Phantom," he said. "Who knows what he's like?"

"By the way, where's Joe?" Robin asked. "Doesn't he usually stop after school? What happened today?"

"Oh, he had to take a special football test," Kevin replied. "The coach is giving it to all the squad members who haven't played football before, or who are weak on the rules."

"Say, that's a break!" Robin exclaimed. "We can

fix up the signals in the studio this afternoon. You and Mike *will* do it, won't you?"

"Sure, but where's Mike?" Kevin asked. "He knows more than I do about wiring and electricity and stuff like that."

"He's probably home by now," Mindy said. "I'll call him and tell him to come on over."

"Mindy and I can start putting Daddy's drawing table and other equipment in the Huddle. Then we can clean the studio," Robin said. "We haven't too much time, you know."

As she went through the hall she heard Mindy say, "Okay, see you in thirty secs, Mike." Together they headed for the studio, followed shortly by Kevin.

"Where will your father work, with us taking over his studio?" Mindy wanted to know. "I'm afraid we didn't think about him when we made our plans."

"Oh, Daddy didn't mind a bit. He's already drawn enough strips for the next three or four days, so we needn't worry. I think it's about the first time in his life that he hasn't been rushing to meet a deadline." She chuckled as she thought of her father's sometimes frantic efforts to get the "Family Scene" to the paper on time.

The studio, located at the far end of the patio, consisted of one large room. Mr. Kane, with the help of Kevin, had built it soon after they had moved to Pacific Point. Although the door was glass and there were two windows at each end, the main illumination came from a large skylight. The walls, painted a soft gray, made a pleasant background for the many old prints which Mr. Kane had collected over the years.

After they had carried the folding drawing table and two or three chairs over to the Huddle, they took down the pictures and maps from the walls. By the time they had swept the floor and pushed a heavy filing cabinet into a corner behind a screen, Michael arrived, armed with an assortment of wires, tools, switches, and electrical supplies.

"I'm sorry I took so long," he said, dumping the stuff on the floor, "but I figured I'd better load up before I came down. It's hard to imagine what Robin has dreamed up!"

"Oh, it's not going to be that complicated," Robin laughed. "I'm no Rube Goldberg. I figure we'll need three two-way buzzers—one in the studio where Jerry will be, another in the house for Daddy, and the third in the Huddle."

"That shouldn't be too hard to rig up," Kevin commented. "But shouldn't you have something to sound a warning if somebody goes through the studio door? You can't see it from the Huddle, you know."

"That's a good idea," Robin replied. "It would alert Jerry, and it might startle the Phantom, too, if it's loud enough."

"How about this idea?" Robin said, after looking slowly around the room. "We can run a string across the door, just about ankle high, and attach Mom's

old dinner bell to one end. When the Phantom trips
over the string, clang goes the bell, out comes Jerry,
and presto, we'll have our man!"

"Who says you're no Rube Goldberg?" Mindy
laughed.

"But what if he doesn't use the door?" Michael
reasoned. "He might come in through the window
over there on the far side of the studio."

"Or even through the one near the Huddle, if he
thinks there's no one home," Mindy said.

"Well, if he comes through that one, Mindy, I'd
see him from where I'm hiding," Robin replied. "Now
about the other one over there—"

She paused as she tried to devise some way of
setting up an alert. While she was thinking, Michael
and Kevin were figuring out how to string the wires
inconspicuously from the studio to the house and to
the Huddle.

"Hey, come here!" Robin finally called out to them.
"I think I've got it!" Her eyes were shining mischievously as the three gathered around her, begging her
to let them in on her plan.

Expecting something complicated, they collapsed
with laughter when Robin told them that it was
simply a matter of being sure the window was locked
so no one could climb through it.

"It's as easy as that!" she said. "The Phantom will
just *have* to use the door or the other window."

It didn't take Michael and Kevin long to complete

their part of the job. Batteries were hidden behind the rose trellis on one side of the Huddle, and when Mindy and Robin were asked to inspect the layout, they couldn't see a single telltale wire. They tested all three buzzers to be sure they worked before Michael temporarily disconnected them.

"All we have to do after the exhibition is to attach these wires to the batteries," he explained. "Is everything set inside, Robin?"

"I think so. Now there's the long wait until Saturday night. I don't think it will *ever* come!"

The next day after school Robin found a chance to talk to Jerry.

"I thought I knew everything that was going on in this town," he said soberly when he had heard about the operations of the Phantom and the plan for the Open House, "but you have kept this a deep, dark secret."

"I suppose we should have reported it sooner," Robin said a little ruefully.

"Well, actually you didn't have too much to go on," Jerry replied, "but I'm glad you finally told me. Any ideas how I might fit into your plan?"

"Yes, Jerry," Robin began in a business-like voice. "Are you on duty Saturday afternoon?"

"No, as a matter of fact, that's my day off, but I haven't planned on doing anything special. Why?"

"If you could come to the Open House that

we're planning, you could wait until no one would notice and hide behind a big screen in the studio. Then, if the Phantom arrives, you'd be in a position to nab him."

"*If* he arrives," Jerry added with a smile. "You know he may not be lured into your trap. But I'm game. I'll be there."

"I'm not even going to *think* of his not coming," Robin declared. "He's *got* to!"

She went on to explain how the buzzers had been set up and how she, her father, and Michael planned to return to the house after appearing to leave for the evening.

"You may have an awfully long wait," Robin warned him, "but your being there ahead of time will mean just one less person who has to sneak back to our house."

"You know, I may get your Phantom before you even arrive," Jerry teased her.

"Well," Robin answered seriously, "that won't make me a bit angry!"

Despite Robin's fear, time, in its usual fashion, moved on, and Saturday morning finally dawned, an unusually warm but clear day. After breakfast Michael drove Mindy over to the Kanes'. He and Kevin planned to drive to Breakwater to pick up the contest entries from the studio people. Mr. Hunter had told him the previous night over the telephone that there were at least ten or twelve entries at Breakwater.

"Some of them are excellent," he had said. "It will be difficult to decide which one is the best."

"Daddy sounded as though he was becoming more interested in the pictures than in nabbing the Phantom," Mindy said with a laugh. "I think you had a real brainstorm when you thought up this show, Robin."

"I'm glad it will serve *some* purpose," Robin replied. "I confess, I'm getting a little worried about the Phantom's falling into our trap."

"You *can't* lose hope now, Sis," Kevin encouraged her. "I'll bet you two banana barges at the Cupboard that you'll get him, and you know what banana barges cost!"

When the two boys had left, Mindy and Robin went out to the studio to wait for people to bring their entries to the contest. It wasn't long before the pictures began to come in, some from local artists, others from the high school students. Three which had been sent from out of town were delivered by mail.

Mindy set up a card table near the studio and pasted a label on the back of each entry with the artist's name and address. Then she passed them to Robin, who took them inside and hung them. There were watercolors, oils, pastels, and even some black-and-white line drawings. Although the girls worked as fast as they could, without the boys to help, a stack of pictures soon collected on the table. Mr. and Mrs. Kane had decided not to look at any of the pictures until they were all hung, so they weren't available to lend a hand. Just as Robin was thinking of calling one of her friends for assistance, Joe and his uncle appeared.

"Am I ever glad to see you two!" Robin exclaimed, mopping her brow. "We're swamped!"

"We figured you might be," Mr. Turner said. "Now tell us what we can do to help."

"I don't seem to be very efficient with this hammer," Robin laughed. "I've hit my thumb more than the picture hangers. Would you take over that job?"

"Glad to," he replied. "I brought another hammer along in case you needed it, so we're all set."

There was barely enough wall space left for the pictures the boys brought back from Breakwater, but by a little crowding they were finally all hung.

"Golly! I wouldn't know which one to pick for the winner," Kevin said as he and Michael looked around the room. "They're all swell."

"Well, not *all* of them, *really,* Kev," Mindy commented slowly, her head tilted to one side as she cast a critical eye over the pictures.

"Oh, *you* have an artistic sense, Mindy," Robin said, "like Mom and Dad. It was completely left out of me, I'm afraid. As they say, I'm no artist. I just know what I like."

"How about you, Mr. Turner?" Michael asked. "Which one would you pick?"

"I agree with Kevin. It's a hard decision," he said,

"but I think I prefer that one of the Spanish ship. Mr. Hunter should be very pleased with such a wonderful show. Will he be here for the Open House?"

"Oh, he wouldn't miss it for the world!" Mindy exclaimed. "I just hope he likes the winner."

After a few minutes more of casual conversation about the paintings, the Turners left, saying they would be back later in the afternoon for the Open House.

When Robin and Mindy went in to change their clothes, they found Mrs. Kane busy in the kitchen.

"Mom, what are you up to?" Robin exclaimed when she saw the array of bottles and fruit on the table.

"It's such a hot day that I thought it would be nice to have a cool drink for our guests," Mrs. Kane explained, "so on my way back from taking Amy to Judy's house, I stopped at the market and got the makings of a fruit punch and plenty of paper cups."

"May we taste it?" Mindy asked. "It's a lovely color!"

"Go ahead, try it, but remember, it isn't iced yet. Does it need more of anything?"

Both girls, after generous samples, pronounced it perfect.

"We can serve it from the long redwood table," Mrs. Kane said. "I have two big bowls, so you and Mindy can be at each end to fill the cups. The boys can bring replenishments from the kitchen. Now run along and dress. It's after three already."

"When are you and Daddy going to pick the winner?" Robin asked. "The pictures are all hung."

"I guess we might as well do it right now," Mrs. Kane said as she took off her apron. "I'll get your father as soon as he's through shaving."

"May we come with you?" Robin asked. "I can't wait to see which one you pick!"

"No, dear, better not. I want this to be absolutely fair, and even though you might *think* you weren't influencing us, after living with you all your life, I can tell what you're thinking simply by looking at your face."

"She's right, Robin," Mindy said. "You just don't have a poker face. Come on. We'll soon know the winner, anyway."

Mindy had brought a pale green sleeveless dress which was a perfect foil for her smooth blond hair. She wore no jewelry except the small gold friendship pin which Robin had given her the Christmas before.

"Oh, Mindy, you always look so beautiful," Robin moaned as she rummaged through her closet trying to decide what to put on. "I feel like an old frump beside you."

"Don't be silly, Robin. What I wouldn't give for your naturally curly hair and that wonderful tan."

"I guess we're never satisfied with our own looks," Robin laughed. "How about my wearing this old yellow linen?"

"It may be old, but you haven't worn it more than

a few times. I adore it. Now what about that jade pin that was your grandmother's? It would be just right with that neckline."

"Jiminy, I'd forgotten all about that!" Robin said, going to her dressing table and opening her leather jewel box. "You're right. It does do something for the dress, doesn't it?"

I'll get her interested in her appearance, someway, Mindy thought to herself. *She's too attractive not to take more interest in what she wears.*

After putting on the dress and pin, Robin slipped into a pair of white shells and took a quick look in the mirror. Then the two friends hurried out to the studio to see which picture would bear the blue star of the winner.

12.

THEY MET KEVIN and Michael on the way to the studio. The two boys had taken a quick swim before changing into clean white ducks and sport shirts. Mr. and Mrs. Kane were just coming out of the studio.

"I declare, that's the hardest job I've ever had!" Mrs. Kane said, taking off her glasses and sitting down near the pool. "There were so many excellent entries."

"You're absolutely right," her husband said. "There were very few pictures in there that didn't show real talent. You young people go on in and see if you don't agree with our choice."

Robin led the way, her eyes glancing quickly around the room to find the blue star.

"There it is!" she cried, pointing to a canvas at one end of the room. "I *love* that one. Let's see who did it!"

"Didn't you look to see the name of the artist when you were hanging the pictures?" Kevin asked.

"I started to, but they came in so fast that I didn't have time after the first few."

She carefully took the picture off the hook. It was a small oil painting showing a procession of hooded monks approaching the mission chapel. Their hands were folded inside the wide sleeves of their dark brown habits, and their heads were reverently bowed. In contrast to their somber garb, the chapel walls were flooded with a warm pink glow from the late afternoon sun. In the background the shore and the sea were painted in soft tones of blue-gray and sand.

"It's Sam's!" Robin cried, recognizing their classmate's name on the label on the back. "I didn't see him this morning! Was he here, Mindy?"

"I'm *sure* he wasn't. You know how shy he is. Maybe he sent it over with someone else. It's *so* beautiful!"

Praise for Sam's picture was unanimous, and Robin ran into the house to try to reach him on the phone to give him the good news. She got no answer, however.

"I *do* hope he turns up this afternoon," she said when she returned. "Do you know, I think this is the first time he's ever exhibited anything in oils. He's always done watercolors before."

She rearranged some of the pictures so that Sam's would be easily spotted as people came through the door. She had just finished when the first guests arrived at the entrance to the patio. She and Mindy took up their positions at either end of the punch table. Mr. and Mrs. Kane remained behind in the studio.

Among the first to arrive was Mr. Hunter. He was delighted when he saw Sam's work. After carefully studying all the other entries, he turned to Mr. Kane.

"I certainly congratulate you on your choice for the first prize, Toby," he said, extending his hand to Robin's father. "That boy certainly shows great promise. I hope he can continue his art studies."

"Sam will be pleased, I know," Mrs. Kane remarked. "The prize will help him buy paints and supplies. I understand money is a little scarce in his family—it's a big one, you know."

Mr. Hunter was soon surrounded by people asking him questions about the film and when they might expect to see it on television.

Joe came over, explaining to Mindy and Robin as he was having punch and cookies that his uncle was sorry he couldn't come, too.

"I guess he felt he'd taken enough time off already," Joe said. "What a schedule he's set for himself! But he's keen to know who the winner is, and so am I."

"It's Sam!" Robin announced. "Remember the picture you specially liked—the monks going up to the chapel?"

"Bully for Sam!" Joe exclaimed. "Where is he? I want to congratulate him."

Sam hadn't arrived yet, and as the afternoon wore on there was no sign of him.

Tony appeared and temporarily disrupted things by telling Mindy he had noticed that her father's car, which was parked out in front, had a flat tire. Michael, overhearing Tony as he was refilling the punch bowls, stopped long enough to dash out to the street, only to realize that he had once again been taken in by one of his friend's pranks! None of the tires was flat, and by the time Michael got back to the party, Tony had disappeared.

Robin kept looking at her watch, anxious to have the last guest leave so that she could put the final details of her plan into operation. Mindy, guessing her thoughts, reminded her that they had plenty of time.

"It's safe to assume the Phantom won't attempt to get into the studio before dark," she told Robin, dropping her voice so that she could not be overheard.

"I suppose so," Robin said petulantly, "but I'm *so* jittery just sitting here doing practically nothing."

"Let's start clearing up," Mindy suggested. "I think everyone's been served, and it doesn't look as though anyone else is coming. Come on! Shake a leg."

The two girls found Kevin and Michael already in the kitchen collecting the empty paper cups in one large box so they could be carted to the incinerator.

"Golly, I'm glad you finally called it a day!" Kevin exclaimed. "Mike and I want to go over the plans again so there won't be any hitch. Is Jerry in the studio?"

"Yes, he strolled in after practically everyone had left," Robin answered, her face serious. "He's hiding behind the screen as we planned. Now you and Mike have to connect the wires while Mindy and I tie the cord on the bell and check the windows—one to be left open and the other locked."

"So far, so good," her brother said. "Next?"

"Next, Mom and Dad and all of us make a great show of going off to dinner with Mr. Hunter," Robin continued, "after we've turned out all the lights."

"As a matter of fact, Mom's been spreading the word all over the neighborhood about our going to the Hunters' for an anniversary celebration tonight," Kevin interposed. "You know how the old grapevine works!"

"I just hope the Phantom was tuned in," Mindy chuckled.

"So, Mindy," Robin continued her instructions, "you and Mike drive off with your father in his car. After a few blocks Mike will get out, sneak down Alvarez Street, and come in the back way to the Huddle."

"Holy cow!" Kevin interrupted her. "Those white duck pants will stand out like headlights! You'd better change into the dark blue shorts you had on this morning, Mike."

"That's a good point," Robin commented. "We don't want to slip up on a single detail. Now, Kev, we'll go in our station wagon, with Mom driving. She can let Dad and me out somewhere along the way. I'm going to take a black scarf and an old raincoat to put on once I'm in the car. Then if anyone does see us on the street they won't recognize us."

"What about Dad?" Kevin queried. "He might be recognized."

"Oh, I forgot," Robin laughed, running out to the hall and returning with one of her father's old beat-up hats and a poncho. "Remember when I wore this back from Rancho Lucia last summer? It will be a perfect disguise for Daddy."

"Well, let's assume now that the stage is set," Michael said in a business-like voice. "You and I are hiding out in the Huddle. Your father is in the house watching for anyone approaching on that side or up the driveway, and Jerry is in the studio. Let's go over the plan from there."

"We're going to signal them with a tiny buzz every five minutes to let them know we're all right and that there are no new developments," Robin said. "If anyone sees anything suspicious, the signal is two short buzzes. Right?"

"Right," the others echoed.

"Do you really think the Phantom might be dangerous?" Mindy asked, her eyes wide with apprehension.

"Probably not," Robin replied in an attempt to reassure her friend. "Up to now he hasn't done anything to cause *physical* harm to anyone, but if he goes into the studio he can be arrested for breaking and entering—I seem to remember that phrase in a police story I once read."

"That should take care of him!" Kevin said. "All we want is to get him out of the way until Mr. Hunter gets the picture made."

As soon as they were sure the way was clear, Robin and Michael, trying to appear completely casual, sauntered across the patio. Michael picked a couple of roses from the yellow rambler behind which the batteries were hidden, and then, purposely dropping one of them, he leaned over and quickly attached the wires, while seeming to pick up the flower. Then he wandered over to the studio where Robin had just finished fixing the bell.

"Oh, Mike, how nice of you!" she exclaimed, immediately sensing his strategy in picking the roses. "These just match my dress. I'm going to wear them

for dinner tonight. Thanks a million!" She talked a little louder than usual just in case anyone was loitering within earshot.

It wasn't long after she had surreptitiously sneaked the poncho, hat, and scarf into the car, and Michael had changed from his white ducks, that the Kanes and Mr. Hunter came into the house.

"If you are all ready, I think we might as well get started," Mr. Hunter said. "Manuela said she'd have dinner for us around eight o'clock."

"Give me five minutes to freshen up," Mrs. Kane replied as she headed for her bedroom, "and I'll be ready to go."

"We're all set any time you are," Robin said, the color in her cheeks high.

"I'll see that the lights are turned off here in the house," Mr. Kane said. "And, Kevin, you check them in the studio."

When they finally headed for the cars there was a great deal of good-natured banter and rather loud laughter. Anyone hearing them would never have guessed the mounting tension they all felt. Robin gave a quick but furtive glance around the patio. There was no sign of life. Tig, who usually occupied one of the chairs near the pool, had been annoyed by the unusual activity of the Open House and had hidden herself away early in the day. Robin had fed Tramp a double ration of his favorite dog food while she and Mindy were in the kitchen, so he was asleep

on Kevin's bed when they left. Everything was quiet
—almost too quiet, Robin thought to herself.

"Mom, you'd better let Dad and me off just before
you get to Palmetto Avenue," Robin said as she tied
the scarf loosely around her head. "We can cross
over and walk back on the other side—it's darker
there."

Kevin, his nose pressed against the side window of
the car, watched for anything unusual along the way.
The streets seemed completely deserted, however.

"I guess everyone's home having dinner," he ob-
served. "Golly, I wish *we* were! I don't like the idea
of Robin and Dad having to go back alone to heaven
knows what!"

"Well, I certainly feel a lot better about it, knowing
Jerry's there," Mrs. Kane said as she brought the car
to a stop so that Robin and her father could slip out
into the night.

"Don't you worry," Robin whispered as she was
leaving. "We'll be okay!"

The two ducked quickly across the street and,
keeping as much as possible in the shadows, headed
back. They hadn't gone far before it started to rain,
and in minutes it was really pouring—a heavy, end-of-
summer downpour. Robin pulled the old raincoat
around her. Her father, head bent against the wind,
took her arm to guide her. At last they reached the
break in the fence and slipped through, pausing only
long enough to look around and assure themselves

that they were not being followed.

"Come on, Dad," Robin whispered urgently. "We don't want to waste a second. You go in the back door and I'll sneak around to the Huddle. Remember, a short buzz every five minutes means everything's okay. Two shorts means an alert."

"I've got it," her father whispered. "Good luck, Robin, and be careful!"

Robin crept along the inside of the willow-sapling fence until she came close to the Huddle. Then, bending over so as to be as inconspicuous as possible, she made a dash across the short open space that separated her from the clubhouse.

When she heard Mike's reassuring voice she realized that she had been holding her breath until her lungs ached. She let out a long sigh of relief as he grabbed her hand and drew her quickly inside. Together they crouched under the windowsill in the dark, holding their heads just high enough so that they could peek outside. Robin felt for the buzzer button and gave the signal to let Jerry and her father know all was well.

"How can we tell when five minutes are up?" Michael whispered. "We forgot that little detail."

"There's a flashlight in the old seaman's chest over there," she answered. "I'll crawl over and get it."

It was dark in the Huddle, and hot and humid, too. The only sound was the rain's beating on the roof. Robin took off the raincoat and edged toward the rear. She had forgotten about a metal stool in the middle of the room—until she stumbled over it. A stinging pain shot up her leg, almost forcing her to cry out, but she stifled the cry by biting hard on her clenched fist.

"Are you all right, Robin?" Michael asked in an anxious voice.

"Yes, I'll be right back. It's only a skinned shin." She groped her way along and finally located the chest and the flashlight.

Now if only the battery isn't dead, she thought as she returned to her post under the window.

It was weak, but there was enough light for Michael to see the hands on his watch.

"It'll last for a while," he whispered. "I only hope we don't have to wait too long."

Five minutes passed. Signals again buzzed. Nothing happened. Ten minutes, twenty, and still nothing but the steady pounding of the rain. Robin's legs were beginning to cramp. She shifted her position to ease them. The abrasion on her leg hurt unmercifully, but there was nothing she could do but bear it. The darkness outside played strange tricks with her eyes. Once she was sure she saw a figure, but Michael assured her it was only an especially heavy sheet of rain blowing around the corner of the building. Their eyes smarted from looking so long and intently in one direction. The studio window seemed to assume strange shapes through the rain.

Suddenly Robin caught Mike's arm and held it tight.

"Look! Over there! The Phantom!"

It was impossible to tell just what it was, but they were certain it wasn't the rain this time. Something looking like a great black ghost moved stealthily, steadily toward the studio.

As Robin watched she raised herself slowly off the floor. Then, seeing the strange form crawl around a corner of the studio, she hit the buzzer two staccato punches and started edging for the door. Almost immediately the clang of the bell rang out into the night. Robin and Michael dashed out of the Huddle and headed for the studio. By the time they reached the door the room was a blaze of light. They found Jerry grappling wildly with a black-caped figure.

Robin let out one piercing scream as she saw the Phantom holding something shining in his right hand. Just then Jerry lost his footing and started to fall. Michael leaped toward the Phantom's upraised arm and grabbed the wrist. This gave Jerry a chance to recover his balance and he soon felled the intruder. As the Phantom went sprawling, an ice pick fell from his hand and clattered to the floor.

Before the Phantom could make another move, Michael was on top of him. With a quick twist he turned his arm behind him in a hammerlock.

The Phantom, lying on his stomach, twisted and turned in a frantic effort to get into a position to defend himself, but he was helpless. The black mask which he had stretched over his head was pulled askew so he could no longer see out of the two small eye slits. Mumbled curses were the only sounds he made.

Hearing Robin's cry, Mr. Kane had immediately dashed from the house. He burst through the door of the studio just as Jerry was putting handcuffs on the Phantom.

"Robin, Robin!" he cried, catching sight of her bloody leg. "Are you all right?"

She threw herself into his arms, tears of relief flooding her eyes.

"Yes, yes! We're all okay! We've caught the Phantom!"

13.

The Phantom Talks

"Y OU KNOW, I've seen a lot of strange characters in my life," Jerry said, straightening up, "but nothing like this! What in the world is it—or who?"

"That's what I intend to find out right now," Robin declared, her composure regained.

She edged gingerly toward the now silent figure, took firm hold of the black mask, and gave a mighty yank.

"Mr. Turner!" she exclaimed in disbelief. "You!"

She gazed in horror at the familiar face, now distorted almost beyond recognition with rage.

"Turner?" Jerry asked after taking a close look at the man.

"Yes, Joe's uncle," Michael said incredulously. "I just can't believe it!"

"Nor I," Mr. Kane said, shaking his head. Then, addressing himself to the figure on the floor, he demanded, "What's behind this horrid scheme of yours? Speak up, man!"

"What do you mean, trying to sabotage Mr. Hunter's picture?" Robin exclaimed.

"I don't know what you're talking about," the Phantom muttered. "I was only trying to play a joke."

"Oh, yes?" Michael said cuttingly. "A fine time for a joke—when you thought no one was home!"

"And what did *this* have to do with the joke?" Robin demanded, picking up the ice pick and brandishing it under his nose.

Before the Phantom could answer, there were sounds of running steps on the patio. Going to the door, Robin was astonished to see Joe, followed by a man whose right arm was in a sling. The little group in the studio fell back as the two came in. They didn't know what was happening.

"There he is!" Joe cried, pointing to the manacled figure on the floor. "*That* is the man who told me he was my Uncle George!"

It didn't take more than a glance at the man who had come in with Joe to recognize him as a relative. The resemblance was unmistakable. He had the same sturdy build as Joe, the same sandy-red hair and deep-set eyes.

"You mean this is the *real* Mr. Turner?" Robin asked incredulously, going over to him. "Yes, you must be—you look just like Joe."

"Yes," he said, looking from one to the other, "I am George Turner, and I'm sure I owe you people an apology. And—" nodding at Jerry "—the police an explanation of tonight's events. You're Mr. Kane?" He went over to Robin's father, his left hand extended in greeting.

"I'm Toby Kane, yes, and this is my daughter, Robin, and over here—Michael Hunter—and Sergeant Smith."

"I'll try to be brief," Joe's uncle began. "This whole unhappy affair started back in Los Angeles about two weeks before I was to move up here to get things ready for Joe's arrival from England. I fell and broke my right wrist—a compound fracture, rather nasty. I had to be hospitalized, and that's where this man came into the picture." He nodded toward the Phantom, who only glared malevolently at the group around him.

"I knew him as Ned Osborn in Los Angeles. We lived in the same apartment building. He'd always seemed like a decent sort of person, quiet and well-spoken, and we sometimes ate dinner together at a restaurant we both frequented. After I fell he came to see me in the hospital, and—"

"And offered to come up to Pacific Point to take care of Joe?" Robin asked.

"That's exactly what he proposed," Mr. Turner continued. "And not having any alternative, I agreed—actually very thankful for his help."

"I'll say you agreed," the Phantom snarled. "You were only too glad to have me help you out of a tough spot."

"But didn't Joe know anything about this?" Robin interjected.

"I supposed he did," Mr. Turner said. "I dictated to Ned a letter for Joe and another for my sister in England, to tell them what had happened and what plans I had made. When I got no replies and couldn't reach Joe by phone, I became alarmed and came up here as soon as they let me leave the hospital."

"The Phantom probably never mailed the letters," Robin said, glaring at him. "Did you?"

"You know all the answers, don't you, kid?" Ned Osborn sneered. "But you can't pin anything on me. I haven't done anything."

"You stole San Andrea's fish and you know it!" Robin persisted. "Besides doing all the other things to upset Mr. Hunter and sabotage his picture."

"You'd better come clean, Ned," Jerry said. "We've already got you for breaking and entering, but if you tell us the rest of the story, Mr. Hunter might be persuaded to drop the other charges. Do you think I'm right, Mr. Kane?"

"I think you can depend on that," Robin's father replied. "Mr. Hunter isn't interested in getting revenge, I'm sure."

"No, he just wants to get on with his film," Robin added. "I know!"

"Okay, okay," Ned muttered. "Undo my legs and get me off this floor. Then I'll talk."

Jerry quickly undid the cord he had tied around his ankles. Ned flopped over on his back awkwardly and finally got into a sitting position.

"It all started five or six years ago," he began. "I had a part in a picture Mr. Hunter was directing. He got me fired—accusing me of trying to steal scenes from the leading man."

He paused as though recalling the situation. A sardonic smile curled the side of his mouth.

"I needed a job, but I couldn't seem to get anything except work as an extra after that. I swore I'd get even someday—somehow."

"So this was your chance," Robin interpolated. "When Mr. Turner broke his wrist, you figured this was a perfect opportunity for you to get close to Mr. Hunter's home and work—here in Pacific Point and at Breakwater."

"Yeah, right away I saw my chance. With this beard I knew Mr. Hunter wouldn't recognize me, and in that monk's getup it was easy to sneak the fish out of the office. No one kept a very close watch on the place. I hid it under my costume until I had a chance to throw it off the dock."

"But why did you tie a string to it?" Robin asked curiously. "Did you plan to pull it up later and claim a reward from the museum? Was that your plan?"

"Maybe, yes; maybe, no!" was Ned's only comment.

"Go on," Jerry urged him. "We haven't got all night."

"Well, when I took a good look around the old Williams place I began to get all kinds of ideas." He stopped, his small eyes almost shut.

"I think I know what he means," Mr. Turner interposed. "That house was once owned by a man who had charge of properties for one of the big studios. As a hobby he built a circular room under the house with all kinds of spooky props and costumes. I discovered a trapdoor leading to it after I'd rented the house last month. I believe I had mentioned it to Ned."

"So that's where he got the ghost costume he wore the night he scared the servants and cut off the Hunters' phone," Robin said, "and probably the swim fins which left the huge tracks we saw in the sand near the house."

"What was his idea of breaking in here?" Joe asked. "More sabotage?"

"Here's the answer to that question, Joe," Robin said, picking up the ice pick and handing it to him. "He was going to slash Sam's picture, and maybe the others, too, so there'd be another delay in the film—

something else to discourage Mr. Hunter."

"But, thanks to Robin, there'll be no more delays," Michael said. "Dad's picture is going to be finished on time."

"Well, I'd better be getting this character back to the station house," Jerry said. "The chief may call on some of you tomorrow for testimony, but tonight you'd better all try to get some sleep."

"Wait just a minute, please," Robin said, her brows furrowed. "There are a couple of things I can't figure out. How did the Phantom get back and forth from Pacific Point to Breakwater if he had no car, and how did he know *we* knew about the fish when he planted the box in the Heap? And also, was it the Phantom who telephoned to instruct Mr. Stern to go to Los Angeles?"

"I think I have the answer to the first part of that," Joe said. "When Uncle George came to the house tonight and I realized Ned was a fraud, we went over every inch of the place together looking for him. His room in the tower showed no sign that he'd ever written a word, and out in a shed in the back we found an old motor scooter. Apparently he used this, when I wasn't around, to get to Breakwater or up to the Hunters'."

"Hmmmm," Robin mused. "Then there's only one answer to the second part of my question. He must have sneaked up to the window of Mr. Hunter's office after everyone else had left the set that night and

listened to him call home. Is that right?" Without waiting for Ned to respond, she went on, "And, being a former actor, he was able to disguise his voice when he telephoned Mr. Stern to direct him to the Westpark Films studio in Los Angeles."

Ned merely nodded his head as he got up to go with Jerry.

When they had left, silence fell on the little group. A great feeling of relief swept over them as they all thought of what might have happened.

Robin suddenly broke the spell, bringing them back to reality. "Daddy, did you phone the Hunters?"

"Good heavens, no!" her father exclaimed. "When I heard you scream, I didn't think of anything but you."

"We've got to call them right away," Robin said. "Come on! They'll be awfully worried!"

It was Mindy who answered Robin's call.

"We've got the Phantom, Mindy. Everybody's okay!" Robin fairly shouted the news. "It was Mr. Turner—only it wasn't really Mr. Turner! Oh, it's all so complicated. I can't begin to tell you over the phone."

"Tell her we'll be right out," Michael suggested.

"We'll be over to your house right away," Robin said.

"And by the way," Michael added, taking the phone from Robin's hand, "we haven't had a bite to eat since noon. Ask Manuela to rustle up some food, will you? Our detectives have to keep up their strength!"

"You're right!" Robin said when he had hung up. "Who knows—tomorrow may bring another mystery!"